The Elixir Deception

By

Margena Adams Holmes

Book cover by Ian Bristow, who captured my vision perfectly.

I'd like to thank my family—Reid, Aerin, Brent, Carter, and Wolfe—for their love and support throughout this journey of writing and editing.

In memory of my furry writing partner, Max. I miss your wet nose nudging my hand off my mouse to pet you.

Chapter One

It was already late, yet the clanking of the machines hadn't ceased, and wouldn't anytime soon. Major Jordan Vance, also known as Prince Jory of Darantha, drove up to the facility to make a late-night visit to see how much of the Elixir they manufactured each day. This manufacturing facility, as well as the one on Ornocto, worked 'round the clock to keep up with demand ever since Kiral Radern and the Elixir War had destroyed all but these two facilities.

The facility director smiled at the late-night visitor, happy at the chance to talk with someone.

"General Frey wants to know if supply is keeping up with demand," Prince Jory said. "Looks like you've got it all handled."

"Yes," said the director. "We keep a full crew on every shift to make sure we can keep up with the demand. The facility on Ornocto does the same."

"I'm traveling to Caledonia and Esray in the next couple of days to see how the reconstruction of the facilities is progressing," Jory said, ignoring the Ornocto comment.

Jory had no intention of going to Ornocto and seeing the facility there. He wouldn't be able to face Deyka after what he'd done in the mission a year ago. That mission—seducing Deyka to get her to help Darantha and give them information on her father—had been one of the hardest missions Jory'd had to do. Even though Samara had known from the beginning what Jory had to do, it'd been hard on her, and she would put her foot down on that trip.

Remembering that mission, he shook his head and ran his hand over his face, trying to erase the memories of that time.

After spending a few minutes with the director and going over the projections for the facility, Jory shook hands with the director and left. It had been a long day and he wanted to get home and crawl into bed with Samara.

Even at that time of night, vehicles filled the streets of Aldra, the capital city on Darantha. Jory maneuvered around a couple of stalled vehicles and headed down a side street to avoid the back-up the vehicles created.

He pulled up to Victoria House a few minutes later. More of a mansion than a house, it was nonetheless much smaller than the palace where the rest of the royal family lived. Walls three meters high surrounded the 3-acre Victoria estate. The grounds were mostly desert rocks and plants, but in one corner was a small green oasis, with trees, grass, and a waterfall, much like the desert plains and forest mountains of the planet.

Jory input the code by hand, not telekinesis, in case anyone nearby had any intentions of getting the code by reading his mind. The gate slid open and Jory pulled in, the gate shutting behind his vehicle. Parking in front of the home, Jory sprinted up the stone walkway to the front door, tapped in his code, and went inside.

The house was dark, but Jory made his way up the stairs with ease. He quietly opened the door to his and Samara's bedroom where he found Samara already asleep. Jory knew she would be, as he had told her he had to stop at the Elixir facility on his way home. He undressed down to his shorts and got into bed next to Samara, being careful not to wake her. He cuddled close to her, burying his face in her sweet-smelling hair, and drifted off to sleep.

Jory awoke the next morning and reached out for Samara, but only found an empty bed. He pulled on his pants and a shirt and went downstairs to find his wife making breakfast for the two of them. Jory came up behind her and encircled her shoulders with his arms, bending down to kiss her neck.

"Good morning, beautiful," he whispered in her ear.

"Good morning," Samara replied. She turned and kissed him. "How was your meeting last night?"

"Informative," he said. "I saw the numbers and the facility is easily keeping up with demand, but I think they'll be grateful

4

when the facilities on Caledonia and Esray are finished. There is a meeting at the base tomorrow regarding the Elixir. Not sure what it's about, but it seems like something big is about to happen. General Frey wants to make sure all the facilities are ready for production as soon as possible."

"You're going to check on the other facilities today?" Samara asked.

"Yeah. Tobi and I will make the trip and be back tonight, hopefully before dinnertime."

Jory's best friend and co-pilot Captain Tobias Kelly had stuck with him through everything that had happened in the last battle. If it hadn't been for Tobias, Jory would have been tortured or even killed in the Elixir War.

After breakfast, Jory jogged upstairs to shower and dress. He put on his uniform and combed his short dark blond hair, running his fingers through his hair to make it not quite so neat and was ready to go.

"I'll have to report to General Frey when we get back, but then I should be able to come home," Jory said.

Jory kissed Samara goodbye, and left for the base.

The Royal Planet Fleet base, on the outskirts of Aldra, had been fairly calm the past few months. The transition of leadership on Ornocto after Jory killed Kiral Radern had been fairly uncomplicated. Radern's daughter Deyka had taken over briefly while elections were held to elect a governor, and Deyka made sure that there were no lingering hostilities. Other than making sure the Elixir facilities were being built, it had been quiet in Darantha's part of the galaxy.

As he entered the Command Center, Jory spotted Tobias's messy brown hair across the room. He made his way around the desks and people to Tobias's computer desk.

"What's on the agenda for today?" Jory asked his friend.

"We're going to Caledonia first," Tobias started. "Then after lunch, we'll head to Esray. We'll meet with General Frey when we get back, then as far as I know, we're done for the day."

"Easy day, I hope," Jory said. "Let's get started."

Tobias logged out of the computer and he and Jory reported briefly to General Frey before heading to the hangar bay.

Jory and Tobias made their way around the various ships and vehicles inside the cavernous hangar bay to their ship near the front. They both checked over the exterior of their ship before going inside to start the ignition sequence. The engines came online and lights came up on the console. After doing their preflight check, they were ready to take off.

"Tyrian One ready to go," said Jory.

"See you this afternoon," said General Frey.

Tobias flipped a switch and the ship lifted off the ground. Jory and Tobias both nudged their controllers forward, the ship moving slowly forward as they did so. Once clear of the hangar, Jory pushed the controller forward more, and they took off into space, going to light speed once clear of the planet's gravity

They arrived at Caledonia half an hour later. They cut to sub-light engines and received clearance to land near the Elixir facility, where they met the governor of Caledonia, Marina Lee.

"Welcome to Caledonia, gentlemen," Governor Lee said, shaking Jory's hand, then Tobias's.

"Thank you, ma'am," Jory said.

"I understand you're just checking on the progress of the facility," the governor said, flipping her dark hair over her shoulder as she walked slowly toward the construction site.

"Yes, ma'am," said Jory. "General Frey wants a report on the progress. We have something planned and we need the facilities up and running."

She gave the men each a hard hat to wear inside, took one for herself, and opened the door. "Right now, the administration building is complete," she said, pointing out the offices. She took them through a set of heavy doors into a bigger room with equipment. "The production area is nearly finished. We're bringing in the machinery tomorrow and getting it set up and we should be ready to start making some preliminary samples by the end of the week. Once they pass Quality and Assurance, we can start making the Elixir in about three weeks."

The governor took Jory and Tobias all through the production area, showing them where everything would finally be set up. Next they saw the storage area, which was also nearly ready, and the packaging area, which was ready to go.

"It looks like you have everything under control," Jory said, smiling. "I know the facility director on Darantha will be happy to hear this."

"Tell them that they can take a vacation soon," the governor told them, laughing.

Jory and Tobias shook the governor's hand as they left, thanking her for her time.

After eating lunch on Caledonia, their next stop on Esray was similar. The facility wasn't as far along as the Caledonia facility, but the director assured Jory that it would be ready in only six more weeks.

Once back on Darantha, Jory and Tobias reported to the general.

"Sir, the facilities are both very close to being operational" Jory told the general. "The facility on Caledonia will be ready in three weeks, and the Esray facility in about six weeks."

"Very good," said General Frey, taking off his silver rimmed glasses and placing them on his desk. "We have that meeting tomorrow after lunch in regard to the Elixir."

"Can you clue us in?" Jory asked.

"I can't at this time. You'll learn all about it tomorrow. Dismissed."

Jory was silent as he thought about the meeting tomorrow. The general's demeanor indicated nothing to worry about.

"Hopefully, it's something good this time," Tobias said.

"Yeah, last time there was a meeting, I got sucked into an impossible mission," Jory replied. "But General Frey promised there wouldn't be anything like that again."

Tobias had some paperwork to do, so he stayed at the base while Jory left. Jory was eager to get home and spend a quiet evening with Samara. General Frey had made good on his promise to make it up to them after the Ornocto mission and let Jory and Samara have time together once they were married. Jory was home almost every night unless he was off-world performing his RPF duties.

Chapter Two

The next afternoon, Jory, Tobias, and the rest of the troops assembled in the conference area for the meeting. No one seemed to know what the meeting was about. There were several men and women whom Jory didn't recognize speaking to General Frey at the front of the room. General Frey went up to the podium and called the meeting to order as the men and women sat down.

"I've called this meeting to update everyone on the Elixir facilities and their progress," the general started. "Our facility and the one on Ornocto have been working overtime to produce enough Elixir for everyone. Members of the public have voluntarily cut back on their consumption of the Elixir so those citizens in the workforce could continue to take theirs to be able to keep the public safe."

The general went over all that had been happening with the facilities, and then called Jory up to the podium to give his report.

"Captain Kelly and I went to both Caledonia and Esray yesterday to check the progress of the facilities there," Jory started. "The Caledonia facility will be ready to start production in three weeks, and the facility on Esray will begin production three weeks later. Both are confident there will be no delays and will be ready on time."

Jory sat down and the general continued.

"Having all the Elixir facilities up and running again will be good news to the planets in all the systems," the general said. "But also because we are in negotiations with the Yarnell System and the Foridian System to start supplying those systems with the Elixir until they have their own facilities built. I've spoken with King Leander and Queen Arika about this, and we think it will be good for all involved."

A buzz rose from the crowd, and Jory and Tobias looked at each other. "Why are we doing this and why now?" Tobias asked.

"I don't know," Jory said, frowning. "My parents didn't tell me anything about this."

General Frey held up his hands for quiet. The murmuring faded.

"If you all will remember your history," the general said. "This is how the current systems started making and using the Elixir, including us. The plant which the Elixir is made from gets shipped to us via freighter, and we make it in our facility. It will be the same with Yarnell and Foridian. We have several pilots who make the runs from Vista, and we'll have several more to take over these new routes as well, starting with shipping the Elixir itself to those systems, then the plants once their facilities are up and running."

"Will this keep our facility running at all hours?" someone asked.

"No, not with the facilities on Caledonia and Esray back in business. The facilities may have to have two shifts, which will create jobs for people."

When there were no more questions, the meeting was adjourned. Everyone stood as the general left the conference area, and the din of voices and chairs scraping rose again as everyone started to leave.

As they left the conference area, Tobias asked, "So, this is a good thing?"

"It could be," Jory said. "More revenue for the systems, not to mention more jobs."

"But will the other people handle it?"

"The effects of the Elixir? The governments will have to oversee everything, make sure no one gets ill, uses it incorrectly, things like that. We turned out okay," he finished with a grin.

"Will you have to sit in on these meetings?"

"Yes, though my father and mother will be in charge of them. Maryllia and Sam will have to sit in, too."

Princess Maryllia, Jory's sister and Lead Interrogator at the base, could easily read minds and see the future and wasn't afraid to speak her mind. She would be sitting in to see if there was any deception on the part of the other government officials.

With their business concluded for the day, Jory and Tobias parted ways and Jory headed back home. He hoped that Samara was back from her duties for the day so they could have a nice quiet evening together.

When he arrived at home, he saw that Samara was indeed back home. He found her sitting at her desk in the office, working at her computer.

"How much more work do you have to do?" Jory asked.

"Maybe another half an hour," Samara said.

"Good, we'll go out to dinner when you're done, then come back home and relax."

Later that evening, Jory told Samara about the meeting he'd had that day.

"We'll have a conference with the governments of both planets with my parents and Maryllia to see about establishing trade routes with the Elixir," Jory said. "If all goes as planned, the trade will start immediately. General Frey will contact you and Maryllia with information to teach members of the governments to use the elixir properly."

"I look forward to it, whenever it happens," Samara said.

***

"We're coming up on the ship, sir," the pilot said into his headset.

"Good," came the reply. "Make sure you don't harm the ship. That cargo is worth a lot to us."

The pilot acknowledged, and a few minutes later the pilot had disabled the smaller ship and had it in the tractor beam. Metz, Keedu's most trusted pilot from Ganta Zay's crew, brought the ship into the hangar bay of the larger ship.

Once the ship was secure, Keedu instructed the pilot of the freighter to power down their engines and step out of the ship. Two men came out a moment later, their hands held up above their heads.

"What is this about?" one of the men demanded.

"I'll ask the questions," Keedu started. "Where are you going with this cargo?"

"We are heading to Sajor, in the Foridian System," the pilot of the freighter replied. "What's it to you?"

"We know what your cargo is," Keedu said, walking around the two men. "We are in need of the food you have in your hold. We will be taking it off your hands."

"But that shipment is meant to go…"

"To us now. If you want to come through this sector again, you will have to pay to pass."

The men were dumbfounded. "We're not going to pay to come through this area. It's open space where you found us. We don't owe you anything."

Keedu stopped in front of the pilot. "You will tell your people that if they want to use that route, they will pay, or we'll fire on you next time and we won't miss. Is that clear?"

The pilot didn't say anything.

"Good. As soon as we've unloaded your shipment, you can go."

Keedu had his men open the cargo hold and unload the crates, which were full of food and other essentials. Ganta Zay's polluted atmosphere made it impossible to grow their own food with any consistency. The smog blocked out the sun most days; not completely, but enough to hinder any growing efforts. What they were able to grow wasn't enough to sustain the entire planet.

The men watched as Keedu's men unloaded the shipment. As the men finished, the pilot ran at Keedu. Keedu reacted, bringing his laser rifle up and shooting the pilot, killing him.

The co-pilot cried out and started toward Keedu. Keedu took aim at him, but didn't fire.

"If you'd like to join your friend, by all means continue," Keedu said. The co-pilot stopped in his tracks. "I will have him loaded into the cargo hold. You can take him back to your planet and let them know that I mean business."

Keedu's second in command, Sayzan, got three other men to help carry the pilot's body into the cargo hold, where they secured it carefully and covered it with a tarp.

"You are free to go," Keedu told the co-pilot. "And remember what I said. We'll know if you come through here again, and you will pay—one way or another."

The co-pilot fired a look of loathing at Keedu, then turned and hurried up the ramp of his ship and shut the hatch. They opened the hangar bay again and the freighter left without interference.

The Gantian ship headed toward Ganta Zay, having finished their patrol of the area for the day. They had gotten a nice collection of food and other items needed to sustain them for a while.

***

The Yarnell System and Foridian System wasted no time in setting up a time to discuss the purchasing of the Elixir and establishing trade routes to the systems. Since the plant was grown on Vista, the conference would take place there. Governor Adké would host the conference in his federal building. Jory and Tobias had checked out the building on their security visit there last year, when the Elixir facilities on Caledonia and Esray had been blown up by Radern's men. It was the most secure building on Vista, with the exception of the governor's building.

All parties involved reworked their schedules to accommodate the conference, which would take place in two weeks. It would take that long to get everything set up, security-wise. King Leander and Queen Arika canceled or rescheduled their meetings, and Maryllia made arrangements for her second in command to take over the workload while she was gone. Jory and Samara would also be there, as would General Frey and his team of advisors. Since Darantha and Ornocto had the biggest facilities, Ornocto would have representatives there as well. Deyka Radern would be there, but only as an advisor to the governor.

When the day came to go to Vista for the conference, Jory and Samara got up early to get ready. Jory worked out with the Virtual Opponent for fifteen minutes before he showered and dressed, then joined Samara in the kitchen for breakfast. After drinking the Elixir, Jory got his things together while Samara got dressed and pulled her long copper-red hair back into a loose twist at the back of her head.

Jory changed into in his dark blue RPF uniform. As he strapped on his weapons belt, he considered leaving them off since this was only a diplomatic visit. He didn't want to be caught without them in the event something did happen en-route to Vista, but would leave them off once they arrived at the governor's estate. Jory could be just as deadly with his abilities as he was with his weapons, and wouldn't need them while in the meetings.

Their staff packed a suitcase for each of them. The negotiations wouldn't take long, but they would be staying at least overnight. A staff member carried the suitcases downstairs and put them in the vehicle. An assistant would accompany them to Vista.

Once Jory and Samara were ready, their driver took them to the base, where they would eventually meet up with his parents and Maryllia. They would all leave from the base in secure transports to Vista. Normally Jory would accompany the transport in his ship with Tobias. Since Jory was part of the diplomatic party, he wasn't allowed to fly his ship, and would be flying in a separate transport, in case anything happened to his parents' ship. Other pilots would take over as escorts on this trip.

Jory never got used to this particular protocol of the royal family. While he understood the need for separate transports to protect the future of the monarchy, he felt he should be the one protecting his family. Tobias would accompany the delegation to Vista as his personal security. Jory trusted Tobias with his life, and used him when he had official duties to perform.

As Jory and Samara walked hand in hand to the general's office, everyone stopped what they were doing to stand respectfully as the couple passed. Even as a major in the RPF, Jory usually didn't get this kind of attention at the base for the most part. The respect was for Samara, who, as a princess now, received a respectful nod as she passed.

They met with General Frey in his office while they waited for King Leander and Queen Arika.

"Lieutenant Vance is finishing up with her replacement in her office," the general said, referring to Maryllia. "She said she'd be here in five minutes."

"My parents should be here soon, too," Jory said.

"The security ship is ready to go whenever we are. We've got our guard ready to go, too." General Frey sat at his desk to get his information together on his electronic tablet.

Maryllia came in a few minutes later with her tablet. "I'm ready to go," she told them. She, too, was dressed in her formal dark blue uniform rather than the purple and black ones they wore every day to the base. Her dark auburn hair, normally left loose or simply pulled back into a pony-tail, was neatly styled into a bun at the nape of her neck.

When King Leander and Queen Arika arrived, security escorted them through the hangar to their waiting ships. Jory and Samara followed with Tobias, Maryllia and General Frey next, and three other government officials made up the entire delegation. They'd been chosen for their specific abilities, mostly mind-reading and seeing into the future. The security detail had strength and seeing into the future abilities.

With everyone secured in their seats in their respective ships, the pilots started the engines and they were cleared to leave the hangar for the four-hour trip to Vista.

***

Rain and wind greeted the delegation on Vista. The ships landed inside the hangar of the Governor's Estate out of the weather. Smaller than the hangar on base on Darantha, it held several smaller ships and a few official vehicles for the governor and his staff. Governor Adké and his security advisor, Ziv Wexler, along with several members of security waited for King Leander and Queen Arika to disembark the ship.

The door opened at the side of the ship and a security guard stepped out first. After taking a quick survey of the area, the king and queen followed him down the ramp.

"Your Majesty," Governor Adké said as he extended his hand to shake King Leander's hand. They shook hands, and King Leander turned to introduce Queen Arika. Jory and Samara came over from their ship with Tobias, Maryllia, and General Frey and were greeted by the governor.

"Major Vance, good to see you again," said the governor, shaking Jory's hand. He greeted Tobias as well, and General Frey introduced Adké to the rest of the delegation.

"As Major Vance knows, this estate is the most secure building on the planet," Ziv Wexler told them. "You'll be staying in the guest wing. You'll find every accommodation you may need there."

"Thank you, Mr. Wexler," said King Leander. "I'm sure we'll be very comfortable."

After getting settled into their rooms, Jory checked on his parents before he joined the security team in the general's room to go over the next day's agenda.

"We'll be meeting with the King of Yarnell and the Governor of Foridian and their delegations," the general said. "I don't foresee anything out of the ordinary happening. It's basically just to get things planned and organized for both the delivery of the Elixir and then the delivery of the plant once their facilities are operational." He turned to Maryllia. "Lieutenant, have you seen anything in the future that is going to happen?"

"I haven't seen anything," Maryllia told him. "It seems straight-forward with them. Things may change once I meet them, but so far, nothing, sir."

The general went over everyone's responsibility for the meetings, just to get everyone on the same page. King Leander and Queen Arika had already been briefed on the meeting. It was their decision and Ornocto's decision to supply the Elixir to the Yarnell and Foridian systems. Everyone expected these meetings to go without any problems.

Chapter Three

Jory got up early the next morning. Without waking Samara, he got out of bed, pulled on his pants, and sat cross-legged on the floor. He closed his eyes and started to clear his mind. He wanted to be aware of everything that happened during the meetings that day. There had been no indication of anything, but his experience with other governments had made him wary of any negotiations.

He reached out using his abilities to see into the future. The first image that came into view was the conference. As Jory delved into that vision, nothing out of the ordinary looked to be happening. He could see all the delegates there, including Deyka. Choosing to focus on her for a moment, he looked and saw that they didn't have any kind of contact, except for business relations during the conference. Taking himself back to the conference, everything looked normal. He turned his focus to after the conference. Everyone got home safely.

"Jory?" Samara's soft voice broke through his meditations. He opened his eyes to see her sitting on the edge of the bed, smiling.

"Hey," he said, breathing in deeply to bring his focus back to the present. He pushed up from the floor to stand and walked over to sit on the bed next to Samara. He kissed her softly. "Ready to start this thing today?" he asked.

"As ready as I'll ever be," she replied with a yawn.

There was a knock on their door. Jory went over to open the door and saw one of Governor Adké's young staff members with a tray of food.

"Breakfast, sir," he said, barely audible, mostly addressing Jory's knees.

Jory took the tray from him. "Thank you very much," Jory said pleasantly. The staff member looked up to give Jory a quick smile and walked away.

The tray was laden with fruits, meats, cheeses, water, and Elixir for the two of them.

"Apparently, breakfast is served," he said, setting the tray down on the bed next to Samara.

After they ate breakfast and drank their Elixir, they got ready for the meeting. Jory dressed in his uniform, and watched Samara get dressed. Samara had picked out her attire for the conference before she left. It was another pantsuit, this time in red, with a gray blouse under the short jacket. She pulled her hair back into a low ponytail and added a clip on each side to help hold her hair in place, applied make-up that set off her green eyes and was ready.

"Beautiful as always," Jory said, gently kissing her cheek. Jory and Samara grabbed their electronic tablets to take notes on, and left their room. The meetings would start at 0900. On their way out, they met up with Tobias and Maryllia.

"General Frey has gone ahead to the federal building to make sure everything is safe for your parents," Tobias told Jory. "I told him we'd wait for you two, and your parents would be there with their own security."

"Good," Jory said. "Maryllia, have you seen anything happening?"

"Nope," she said. "Everything seems pretty straightforward so far."

"I didn't see anything, either," Jory told her.

They walked across the compound to the transport waiting to take them to the federal building. After a short drive, they arrived at the building and were directed to the conference room. The dark rectangular table, with about twenty chairs around it, took up most of the room. Windows at one end of the room let in light now that the rain had stopped. Jory and Samara took their place next to General Frey along one side of the table and the rest of the delegation followed. King Leander and Queen Arika would take the seats at the head of the table along with Governor Adké and

Ziv Wexler. The door opened again, and Deyka Radern walked in with Ornocto's new Governor, Max Kyle.

Looking as beautiful as she did when Jory last saw her, Deyka looked around the room and her eyes settled on Jory and Samara. Jory gave her a nod of his head, and Deyka smiled, then turned her attention to her Governor again. Deyka and Jory had come to some sort of an understanding. Deyka knew that Jory had to kill her father during the Elixir War, and while they would never be friends again, they would be cordial to each other if they ever met in the course of their government's interactions.

Samara, Maryllia, and Tobias had also watched Deyka come into the room. All three of them turned to look at Jory, who frowned. "I hadn't even thought about her until we started talking about this conference," he told them, answering their unspoken question. "I have no intention of starting a personal conversation with her at all. Business only." Breaking protocol, Jory reached out and squeezed Samara's hand. Even though it had been his assignment to get back together with Deyka, he had played the role well and convinced everyone that he was in love with her. It had been an assignment he hadn't wanted to do, and it had hurt the people he loved.

Before any of them could say anything else, the door opened and everyone stood as King Leander, Queen Arika, and Governor Adké entered the room, followed by Governor Paden Oxmoor of Foridian and King Gaius of Yarnell. Accompanying King Gaius were his advisor, Zaine Ortix, and a security guard. Governor Oxmoor brought his security advisor, Malin Garrick, and the general of his military troops.

Once they finished the introductions, everyone took their seats. Governor Adké stood and called the conference to order.

"I'd like to welcome everyone to this conference," Governor Adké started. "These negotiations are to hammer out the details of distributing the Elixir to the Yarnell and Foridian Systems, and to help them build their own facilities to manufacture the Elixir themselves. We will discuss and plan shipping routes to the systems and who will be in charge of the routes. Does anyone have any questions?"

"It seems all pretty straight-forward to me," said King Gaius, looking around the table. The other delegates nodded.

"Then let's get to it." Governor Adké sat down and the conference began.

"I think the first thing that needs to be done is King Gaius and Governor Oxmoor should drink the Elixir so they can find out for themselves what happens when one drinks it," said King Leander.

"We've actually both tried it," Governor Oxmoor replied. "In preparation for this conference we drank it yesterday. Everything seemed clearer, and we seemed to be stronger and could catch glimpses of what was in each other's mind."

"With instruction, you'll learn to use those abilities to their full extent," Governor Adké told them. "Most people learn through years of schooling, but since this will be new to everyone on your planets, we will instruct some of your teachers to use their abilities and then pass on what they learn."

"This will open up many career opportunities for your people," Deyka said. "Not only to teach them how to use their abilities, but also use their abilities for their jobs."

"Princess Samara, who is an instructor at the Academy, and Lieutenant Maryllia Vance, Lead Interrogator with the Royal Planet Fleet, will teach your government leaders how to use their abilities and how to apply them to your careers," General Frey said.

After getting the details of using the Elixir taken care of, they got to the more important concerns of building the facilities and transporting the Elixir to the planets. Once the facilities on Caledonia and Esray were functional, they would join Ornocto and Darantha in shipping the Elixir to Yarnell and Foridian. The foreman and directors working on Caledonia and Esray would move to Yarnell and Foridian to help start those buildings.

As of now, the Elixir would only be used on Foridian and Yarnell, not on other planets in the system. Once the Elixir manufacturing facilities were built on Foridian and Yarnell, then it would be distributed to the other planets in the system, and those planets would then start teaching their citizens on how to use the Elixir and control their abilities.

"We've got the plans to transfer to you for you to start on your buildings," General Frey said. "So you can start right away on getting the building materials together."

"I think I speak for both of us when I say we'll be happy for the help," King Gaius said.

"Absolutely," Governor Oxmoor agreed.

They moved on to the shipping details.

"We'll send shipments of the Elixir once a week," King Leander said. "With Ornocto also sending shipments, that should take care of your needs for the week."

"Once Caledonia and Esray start making the Elixir again, they can also add shipments, too," Jory said. "They've already planned on that."

"What about Ganta Zay?" Governor Oxmoor asked. "The direct route to Foridian is almost entirely a no-fly zone because of the pirates."

"How do you get through the area?" General Frey asked.

"We have to take the longer route around Startia. It's a little out of the way, but safer. We've tried flying near Startia on the direct route, but the Gantians expand their territory at will, so we just avoid it altogether."

"Shouldn't be a problem for us to do the same," Frey said.

Jory noticed Maryllia shift in her seat. He followed her gaze across the table to Governor Oxmoor and his advisor. She had the look of trying to read someone's mind.

He leaned across Samara, and whispered to his sister, "What's wrong?"

"Maybe nothing," Maryllia replied. "But once we started talking about the shipments, something flashed in my mind regarding Foridian."

"Should you bring it up?"

"Yes, I think I will bring this up," Maryllia said, and she raised her hand slightly. "Sorry to interrupt," she told the delegation. "But I have an issue with the Foridian delegates."

"What's this all about?" Governor Oxmoor asked.

"Please," Governor Adké said, holding his hands out to Oxmoor to calm him. "As you know, we asked Lieutenant Vance to this conference to help us vet out all interested parties in the Elixir Trade because her ability to sense any deception is excellent."

"I know of her reputation as an Interrogator," Governor Oxmoor said, nodding cordially to Maryllia.

"During the discussion on shipments I sensed something, albeit briefly, of some kind of deception. I can't pinpoint it." Maryllia said.

"What do you need from us?" Oxmoor asked.

"We'd like your permission for her to read your mind," General Frey said, looking to Governor Adké for permission.

"I'll allow it," Adké said.

"We have nothing to hide," Governor Oxmoor said. "Of course."

Maryllia looked directly into the governor's eyes, ready to read his thoughts. She could easily delve into his mind, searching for any thoughts. She found his thoughts on the Elixir, on the conference, and on his wife back home, pregnant with their first child. She searched through his thoughts on the Elixir, sorting through them, but found nothing that indicated he was deceiving them. She only found his concerns about Ganta Zay, which she already knew about.

"I apologize for the intrusion," Maryllia said. She looked at General Frey and Governor Adké. "Nothing deceptive in his thoughts."

Next she looked into Malin Garrick's eyes. He seemed a little more reluctant to have his mind probed, but nonetheless she looked into his mind effortlessly. She also found his concerns about Ganta Zay, but nothing else. Literally nothing else. It was like reading in the dark. She broke through his blocks, though it was still hard to read everything.

"It's difficult to read his mind," Maryllia stated.

"What are you hiding?" King Gaius shouted at Garrick.

"I'm not hiding anything!" Garrick said forcefully.

"Then why can't the best interrogator in the galaxy read your mind?" Gaius asked

"I won't have my advisor berated by you," Oxmoor interjected.

"Gentlemen," Adké said, his hands up to stifle the shouting. "Let Lieutenant Vance speak."

Maryllia turned to General Frey. "It was like I couldn't see anything. I saw his concerns with Ganta Zay, but then—nothing. I was able to read more of his thoughts as I explored, but it was challenging. I've never met anyone who could hide their thoughts without using the Elixir as well as Mr. Garrick seems to be able to do."

Governor Oxmoor turned to his advisor. "*Are* you hiding anything?"

Garrick cleared his throat. "As your advisor, I know many things that shouldn't be out in the open. Things about you, about our government, that I didn't think you'd want known." He turned to Maryllia. "I've learned to hide my thoughts well, being the advisor to Governor Oxmoor, since we do live in such close proximity to Ganta Zay."

"You can trust them, Malin," Oxmoor assured his advisor.

Garrick let Maryllia search his mind again. This time, she found everything that she had seen in Oxmoor's mind, including the pregnancy, which the governor had not announced to anyone yet, and more detail of what she'd had to dig for in the previous attempt at reading Garrick's mind. She looked for anything related to Ganta Zay just to be sure and saw his thoughts on the pirates and the no-fly zone. After spending a few more minutes searching, she took a deep breath and closed her eyes to break the connection with Garrick.

"Thank you," Maryllia said. "Again, I apologize for the intrusion."

"Is everything satisfactory?" Governor Adké asked.

"Yes," she told them. "Nothing to worry about. I guess what I got earlier was just their concerns with Ganta Zay."

They turned their attention back to their host.

"So we've got the shipments covered," Governor Adké stated. "Now how to get them there."

"We've got a couple of pilots who make the runs from Darantha to Caledonia and Esray already," said General Frey. "We can find a couple more pilots and add a route to Yarnell and Foridian, no problem."

"We also have a couple of pilots in mind for the routes as well," Governor Kyle of Ornocto replied.

Distribution was scheduled to start in a week. General Frey would inform the pilots and get the shipments ready. The routes to and from the planets were agreed upon. The only thing left was to schedule time to instruct those who would be teaching the people how to use their abilities. The governments would send teachers to the Academy where Samara taught, and she would give a special lesson after-hours for a couple weeks, with Maryllia also helping in the class.

The conference took most of the day, with a short break for lunch, getting all the minor details sorted out with each government.

"We look forward to starting the lessons right away,' said Governor Oxmoor.

"We'll be in touch tomorrow to set up times," General Frey said. "Princess Samara will have to clear her schedule to teach these lessons."

King Gaius would send some of his staff and instructors from the college on Yarnell to learn how to use the Elixir abilities.

With the conference adjourned, everyone stood up to greet and speak to each other. Jory didn't want to stick around any longer. He looked for General Frey to let him know he and Samara would be out in the courtyard. He found General Frey and Maryllia in the corridor speaking together in hushed tones to avoid any others from hearing them.

"Did you sense anything else out of the ordinary?" General Frey asked her.

"No, sir," Maryllia said. "Just that brief moment about their concerns with Ganta Zay and which routes to use."

"What's with this Ganta Zay?" Jory asked as he walked up to them.

"Ganta Zay is a little known planet near Foridian that is similar to a penal planet," General Frey started. "Pirates, criminals, people who don't want to be found, hide out on Ganta Zay. The government there is corrupt, probably run by pirates. That was a concern of mine as well, but we'll have our best pilot with our most secure ship deliver to Foridian."

"I've heard of it, but didn't think it was that significant," Jory said.

"It's a small planet on the edge of the Monta Nesta System. The Nestians try to keep it under some kind of control, but aren't always successful. We'll investigate them a little more before we start the shipments to Foridian."

Jory, Samara, Tobias, and Maryllia left the conference room to go to the courtyard.

"We'll have our work cut out for us for the next several months," Maryllia said.

"Good," said Jory. "It's been too quiet lately."

"It will be nice to teach full-time, even if it's just for a couple of weeks," said Samara.

"Getting bored with being a princess already?" Jory joked.

Samara laughed. "No, but I've always loved teaching."

***

Once back in his room after the meeting, a pale-haired man with the skin to match sat on his bed, shaking. He hadn't known that Princess Maryllia would be at the meeting. He *should* have known, since she was the most trusted Interrogator in the RPF, and King Leander's daughter. He hoped that he'd been able to hide what he'd been thinking fast enough so that the princess didn't pick up on what he had planned. If his plan went well, he'd be powerful enough to take over things on Ganta Zay.

***

Several days later, Keedu got word that there was something big happening with Foridian.

"It seems like they are in negotiations with Darantha," Sayzan told him. "Darantha has an Elixir that gives them certain abilities."

"What abilities?" Keedu asked, intrigued.

"I'm not sure," Sayzan said. "But they must be powerful since Foridian wants it."

Keedu thought about that. He turned on his computer and looked up the Elixir. He knew of Darantha, but hadn't heard about this Elixir. The more he read, the more he wanted it. It could help them gain more control of the area.

The Nestians had tried to control Ganta Zay, but every time they tried to intercept Keedu's ships in the area, they were destroyed or severely disabled and had to turn back. The Nestians made the space around Ganta Zay a "no-fly" area to keep the peace, but travelers from other planets and systems who didn't know about Ganta Zay were confronted and hijacked if the Gantians could use their cargo.

The thought of getting this Elixir excited Keedu. He turned to Sayzan. "I'm going to contact Darantha and get that Elixir one way or another."

Keedu figured he'd start with King Leander of Darantha. He tried contacting him, but could not get past the idiot screening the communications, so he contacted the general of the Royal Planet Fleet.

After making some threats, Keedu was put through to General Frey.

The men sat and listened to the conversation between their leader and the general of the RPF. Keedu, pissed that they weren't invited to the conference on Vista, tried the diplomatic way first.

"We will trade our duratatium for the Elixir," he told the general.

"We will not trade with you," the general said firmly. "We don't need the metal."

"Then we'll buy it from you. We will pay you handsomely for it."

"We will not trade nor sell it to you," General Frey stated. "We know your reputation and we will not be a part of your illegal activities. We don't deal with criminals."

That angered Keedu. Here he was, trying diplomacy, which didn't come easily to him and the general didn't seem to appreciate it. He knew that the general wouldn't respond to intimidations, but Keedu had reached his limit.

"If we don't strike a deal to get the Elixir, you will pay for your lack of negotiating with us."

"No deal," Frey said firmly.

"We will get the Elixir, one way or another," Keedu threatened.

With that, he hit the button on the console, disengaging the communication.

"How do you plan to get the Elixir?" asked Sayzan.

"I know someone on Foridian," Keedu said. "I'll contact him and ask for his help."

Chapter Four

The ship landed in Caledonia's hangar bay. The engines powered down and the pilot picked up her bag and walked down the ramp, her long, pink-streaked blonde hair blowing in the breeze from the open hangar bay doors. Evalycer Nicholls looked around and found the foreman sitting at his desk, waiting for her arrival. She walked over, took off her jacket, and sat down in the chair with a heavy sigh, dropping her bag on the floor next to her.

"What's wrong with you?" asked the foreman.

"Well," she started. "Once your facility is up and running, I'm out of a job again."

"I'm sure you'll find something right away," he said, looking over the shipping invoice on the electronic tablet on his desk.

"Maybe," she hesitated.

"Aren't you the one that left the RPF security team to be a pilot-for-hire?"

"Yes, and this job has been great, but I expected something else to come up by now."

The foreman left to go check the shipment against the invoice. Evalycer ran her hands over her face and rubbed her eyes. The trip from Darantha to Caledonia wasn't a long one, but she had stayed up far too late last night playing a card game with several other pilots. She was looking forward to dropping her shipment off, flying back home, and crawling into bed.

The foreman came back a few minutes later. "Everything looks good. Once it's unloaded you can be on your way."

"Great, thanks," she said, a little more effort in her voice.

It took about half an hour for the workers to unload the shipment. During that time Evalycer drank a cup of Stimulating Tea to wake her up for the trip back home. With a wave to the foreman, Evalycer left the office and got back on her ship.

"See ya next week," Evalycer said into the mic as she got permission to leave the hangar bay.

"Safe travels," the foreman told her, and Evalycer left the hangar and headed toward home. Once out of Caledonia's airspace, she engaged the hyper-drive and she arrived back on Darantha an hour later.

She flew in to Aldra and landed at the Hot Shot Spaceport near the center of the city. Once she had disembarked her ship, she went to her land rover and threw her things into the back. Before she could get in, however, she had a message from General Frey on her communicator.

"Come see me when you're back from Caledonia," the message read.

"Urgh," Evalycer growled, but she got into her vehicle and drove to the base to meet with General Frey.

She arrived at the base and pulled out her entrance pass. She was not an active member of the RPF and therefore had to show her identification and pass to get onto the base. She had held the rank of lieutenant as a security member and had worked as an interrogator and as a guard. When it had been time to re-up last year, she declined. At twenty-five years old, she'd had enough of the military life and wanted to do her own thing. Now, a year later, she had more freedom to fly what and where she wanted, though she did a lot of contract work with the RPF because of her reputation as someone with integrity and ethics, and using her abilities. She was well trusted by General Frey.

She parked her vehicle in the visitor's parking area and meandered through the base, looking around and catching up with people she used to work with. She finally made her way to the General Frey's office. She knocked on the door and the general beckoned her in.

"Lieutenant Nicholls," General Frey started as he stood up.

"Sir," Evalycer replied, cringing at the use of her former rank. Either the general didn't notice, or ignored it. She shook the general's outstretched hand. "What can I do for you?" she asked.

"Please have a seat," the general said, indicating the chair in front of his desk. She sat down and General Frey pushed a button on the communicator on his desk and asked for two members of the RPF to come into the office. Evalycer stood up when Prince Jory and Princess Maryllia entered the room and gave them a respectful nod and they all sat again.

"I know your contract with Caledonia is coming to an end soon," said General Frey. "I have another contract for you, if you're interested."

Evalycer sat up a little straighter. "Go on," she said.

"We've just come back from a conference on Vista to establish trade routes to the Yarnell and Foridian systems for the Elixir."

"We're going to be supplying them with the Elixir?" Evalycer asked.

"Until they get their own facilities built, which could take a few months or longer. Lieutenant Vance and Princess Samara will be instructing teachers from both systems on how to use their abilities once they start taking the Elixir, who in turn will teach the people on their own planets. We need someone to take the Elixir to those systems and your name was at the top of my list. Do you want the job?"

"Hell yeah!" she said. "Which route?"

"I think I'll be sending you on the route to Foridian. Your particular set of skills will be useful on the route."

"'My particular set of skills'?" she asked. "What does that mean?"

"There is another system near the Foridian System that has, shall we say, some undesirable inhabitants that could be a problem."

"Like…"

"Pirates," Jory said. "They have threatened us that they will take the Elixir from us."

"You'll have to fly around Startia to avoid Ganta Zay," Frey told them.

Evalycer's heart stopped. Fly around Startia? That would complicate things. She hoped her concern didn't show on her face. "Well, that will make things interesting, won't it?" Evalycer said. Her meaning was clear.

"We'll pay you well for this route. Lieutenant Vance will head the security team on your ship, and Major Vance and Captain Fletcher will be the escorts."

"Keeping it all in the family, huh?" Evalycer asked, looking at Jory. She knew of his reputation as a pilot, and she had worked with Maryllia on the security team. This would be the best team to fly the route to Foridian, and the best team to keep Evalycer out of harm's way. "I'll do it," Evalycer said. "When do we start?"

"Next week," said General Frey. "We'll get someone to cover your runs to Caledonia for the last three weeks, and you'll still be paid in full, since that was part of the contract," the general added when Evalycer started to protest.

"Okay," she said.

"We can meet later today or tomorrow and talk about the security crew," Maryllia said.

"I look forward to it," Evalycer said, and they all stood to leave. Evalycer shook hands with everyone and left the office.

Evalycer fairly bounced as she left the base, eager to start this new job. The pay was good and she would be working with the best of the best. Evalycer knew that Prince Jory would recruit Tobias for the team as well, and having Princess Maryllia was also an asset. The job with Caledonia had been monotonous and solitary. The highlight was getting to speak with the foreman on Caledonia. She looked forward to the possible excitement of this job. The drawback of course was having to fly past Startia.

Once she got home, she contacted some people. She would need a co-pilot for sure, and perhaps a small crew. Evalycer could handle the ship on her own, but if it got as dangerous as she thought it would, she'd need some backup besides the two escort fighters. She knew Princess Maryllia would be on the ship, but a couple other people couldn't hurt.

***

"What do you know about Evalycer Nicholls?" Jory asked Maryllia as they left the general's office.

"She's a great interrogator," Maryllia started. "She was one of my go-to interrogators when she worked here as she can read minds very well. She also worked security. I'm surprised you two never crossed paths, as much as you got put on security detail for your discipline," she said with a smirk.

"I think I've seen her, but never worked with her."

"She's good with a blaster. Bit of a hot-head, though. She'll shoot first and ask questions later. She keeps to herself for the most part."

"I can see why General Frey wants her on this particular route," Jory chuckled. "Does she follow directions well?"

"She did when she was under my authority. She was a good officer, she just wanted to do her own thing."

"I'll see you later," Jory said, and he headed out of the hangar bay to his vehicle.

Jory arrived at home a few minutes later. He found Samara in the office, making up her lesson plan for the delegates she'd be teaching.

"This is going to be such a remarkable task," Samara said. "I know I teach students how to control their abilities now, but teaching a whole new planet how to use their abilities is just astounding."

"I knew you'd be the right person for this duty," Jory said. He walked around behind her to see the computer screen. "What have you got so far?"

"I've taken my lessons from the Academy and revised them to accommodate adults. I've also looked back through our historical archives to see how people reacted when they first started taking the Elixir, and I'm coming up with my own lessons for that as well."

"Sounds like the lessons will be in good hands," Jory said, encircling her shoulders with his arms and kissing her neck. "Ready to call it a night?" he asked.

Samara saved her work and turned off her computer. She turned around and said with a smile, "I'm all yours."

Chapter Five

Samara awoke before Jory the next morning. Excited to start her work day, she threw the blankets off her, being careful not to wake Jory. She dressed quickly and went downstairs to make breakfast for Jory and herself. She would finalize her lessons, then meet with Maryllia at the Academy before they both headed to the base for the lessons with the delegates.

She went in to wake Jory up so they could eat their meal together. He dressed quickly, and came into the kitchen to eat. After they drank their Elixir for the day, Samara left for the Academy while Jory went to the base.

Maryllia was already at the Academy waiting for Samara. Samara walked up the steps and she and Maryllia walked to Samara's classroom.

"We have plenty of Elixir at the base," Maryllia told her. "You're going to teach them how to use their abilities; I'm just there to make sure everyone stays in control."

"I appreciate that," Samara said. "It will be a little different with adults, because they haven't been drinking it since they were fourteen years old and grown up with it."

Samara got what she needed from her classroom, and she and Maryllia drove over to the base together. General Frey had one of the larger conference rooms set up for them. Samara turned on her computer and while that booted up, she repositioned the tables and chairs into more of a classroom arrangement. Once everything was in order and the computer was up, Samara pulled up her lessons and got them up on the main monitor in the room. Twenty cans of the Elixir sat in the corner.

Samara wasn't nervous, but there was a lot riding on how this turned out. She was about to help change several million people's lives with her instruction, something she'd never attempted before.

Samara stood stock-still in the middle of the room, mind blank, staring into the corner of the room.

"Hey," Maryllia said, snapping her fingers. "Are you all right?"

Samara turned to Maryllia and returned her focus to the classroom.

"Just a little nervous," Samara said.

"You'll be fine," Maryllia told her.

Samara smiled, and finished setting up her classroom.

Teachers, instructors, and other government officials started to arrive half an hour later. General Frey greeted them individually and directed them to the conference room. The heads of planets were not in attendance. They would learn to use their abilities from their private instructors that attended the classes.

There were twenty people total and once everyone was settled, Samara started her lesson. She gave each person a can of Elixir to drink. As it started to take effect, she described what would happen and what they would soon be feeling.

"You will soon start feeling like you are more aware of things around you," Samara started as she walked around the room to observe. "Some of you will feel different things, because not everyone has the same abilities. You should all have telekinetic abilities, but some of you will have strength ability, some will be able to read minds, or see into the future."

"Ma'am? How do you know which abilities you have?" asked Zaine Ortix, the advisor to King Gaius of Yarnell.

"It will take about a week for your abilities to fully surface," Samara told them. "But you should have an idea by the end of the lessons today. If your ability is strength, you'll know when you open a door or shake someone's hand."

"I'd like to apologize in advance if I crush anyone's hand," Zaine joked. Everyone laughed.

"It will take some getting used to," Samara said, smiling. "In these lessons you'll learn to recognize the signs of your abilities and use them properly."

While the class waited for the Elixir to take effect, Samara told them the history of the Elixir.

"A thousand years ago on the planet Vista," she began. "A plant was discovered by a traveler. He was hungry and ate the leaves of the *Venturis Visum* plant. After eating the leaves, he felt much stronger. He found he could also see the future as he relaxed for sleep. He had seen the plants all over in his travels. Thinking that they would keep him strong on his journey, he kept eating them. He noticed that after a week of eating the leaves, he felt stronger and seeing the future came much more easily for him. He also noticed that he could make items do his will, submit to his command. He wasn't much of a scientist, but he knew he was onto something. Once he reached his destination, he told his doctor friend about his discovery.

"After some research, the doctor made public his findings. The government took over and made it available to everyone, buying the recipe from the doctor and his friend. The ability one has depends on your genetics. Mind-reading and seeing into the future are born from intelligence; speed and strength are abilities that could develop in those with physical heredities, and nearly everyone will have telekinesis ability. Children start drinking the Elixir at the age of fourteen, and once their abilities start to surface, their education takes on a new meaning and tailored to the ability."

As she walked around the classroom, Samara noticed items on the tables started to twitch as the telekinesis abilities started to emerge. It was almost comical as the items started to fall off the tables and everyone bent down to pick them back up. After this happened multiple times, she asked everyone to hold in their hand whatever was on the desk, or to just leave it where it fell. She wondered if it was like this for the teachers who taught the younger kids to use their abilities, and thought she maybe should have consulted with them about this.

Maryllia kept her eye on things during the lesson. She read the minds of the people there, making sure no one had any intentions to do anything hurtful during the lessons. Most of the delegates grew frustrated in their attempts to use any ability that may be forming.

"It's not going to happen in one day or overnight," Maryllia told them. "You have to give it a chance to form."

At the end of the lessons, several of the delegates noticed which abilities were forming in themselves.

"When you wake up tomorrow morning, drink your Elixir right away," Samara told them. "By the time you get here, you should notice your abilities starting up again. Once you start drinking the Elixir regularly, you won't have a drop in ability in the morning. If you don't drink it at all that day, however, your abilities will diminish by the evening. It's important to drink it in the morning to keep them strong."

Samara dismissed the class. Everyone thanked Samara for her instruction and looked forward to the next day's lessons. The delegates would stay on Darantha during the two-week learning period. Once the lessons were over, they would take what they learned back to their home planet and teach their people. Higher education schools had already added curriculum to their programs to teach students how to use their abilities, just like on the other planets. Younger students would start learning about their abilities and drinking the Elixir at age fourteen, and those schools would add classes as well. Adults would have the option to attend programs at the school of their choice.

"Thanks for your help today," Samara told Maryllia as they walked down the corridor of the base.

"My pleasure," Maryllia said. "It was pretty interesting, actually. It kind of took me back to my school days, learning how to use my abilities. I wonder if we looked as silly as they did with everything falling off the tables."

"I'm sure we did," Samara grinned. "See you tomorrow."

Maryllia waved and proceeded to General Frey's office to report how the class went.

Samara found Jory and Tobias in the lounge of the base.

"How'd it go?" Jory asked, kissing Samara quickly on the cheek.

"I think it went well," she said. "They'll all get the hang of it by the middle of the week."

Jory and Samara said their goodbyes to Tobias. Jory drove to the Academy so Samara could pick up her vehicle, and they both headed toward home.

The next day went a little more smoothly for Samara and her class. The delegates had drunk their Elixir before coming to class, and they were getting better at controlling their abilities. Items didn't jump around on the tables and fall off like the previous day. By the third day of lessons, Samara was able to determine which abilities each person had. Once she verified her impressions with Maryllia and a couple other instructors, they separated into groups according to their abilities. Maryllia took on the mind-readers, Jory took the students with strength and speed, and Samara kept the seers.

***

Maryllia took the eight people in her group into a smaller room across the corridor from the conference room. She had them sit in chairs in a semi-circle facing her.

"I want all of you to clear your mind," she started. "Breathe deeply and evenly. Once you've done that, I'll instruct you on how to focus more to read the minds of others."

Maryllia waited until she thought everyone had done as she'd said. They all looked relaxed and ready to continue. She put them into pairs to work with each other.

"I want one of you to read the other's mind. Concentrate on the person's thoughts. As you get into their mind, stretch out and see how much you can read."

She watched as her students concentrated on their subject. Maryllia walked around the group, stopping next to each pair to read what they were reading. It seemed that the group could read minds fairly easily.

"Now, I want you to go deeper into their mind, trying to break through any walls you come across."

Only two in the group were able to break through any defenses the other put up. The rest seemed frustrated by their lack of ability to do so.

"It's okay," Maryllia told them. "It sometimes takes years of practice to do that. Once you get more in control of the ability, you will find you can read minds more easily and see what others don't want you to see."

"How long did it take you?" one of the students asked.

"It took me a year to do it consistently," Maryllia told him. "It wasn't always easy, and it's something you have to work at. We'll work more on this tomorrow."

***

Jory had better luck with his group. He directed them how to use their ability and call upon it when they needed it.

"When you need your abilities, it's the same as when you command that the lights turn off or you unlock a door," Jory told his group of five people. "Command your arms to be strong." Jory brought out a length of metal pipe about a meter long and gave it to one of the women in the group. "I want you to bend the pipe."

The woman took the pipe in her hands and tried to bend it. It didn't budge.

"Now, *tell* your arms to bend it. Concentrate on your muscles, telling them to do it."

The woman again made to bend the pipe, and it bent easily this time. Her eyes widened in surprise and a smile spread across her face as the other students applauded.

"It's the same when you use your telekinetic abilities. After practice, you should be able to call upon your abilities just by thinking it."

***

Samara's students learned quickly how to see into the future. She taught them how to clear the mind and relax to use that ability. She guided them into a meditative state, and all of them were able to see the future, albeit briefly and only about an hour into the future.

"As with all the abilities, it will take time to use them consistently," Samara told them. "Practice tonight, and tomorrow we'll continue the lesson."

Maryllia and Jory kept their groups the next day and for the rest of the week. By the time the lessons were over the following week, the delegates' confidence in their abilities had grown. Samara felt that the delegates would be fully capable to teach their people on their own planets how to use their abilities. The teachers were especially quick in learning how to direct their abilities, thanks to Samara's instruction.

***

Evalycer awoke with a start. She'd been dreaming about pirates. Not the pirates that you'd find in outer space, but pirates from long ago, that would ride the high seas and take over and pillage other sailing ships for gold. What had made her dream about that? Oh, yes, she remembered, the contract job she was about to start for the RPF. She tossed off the blankets and hurriedly got out of bed.

That job starts today. She padded to her kitchen to start breakfast for herself. She looked in her refrigerator and noticed that the shelves were quite bare. She rummaged around and found some meat and fruit. She heated the meat up as she grabbed a bottle of water and a can of Elixir. When the meat was cooked through, she sat at the table and ate quickly.

After drinking her Elixir, Evalycer showered and dressed in her work clothes, which consisted of a pair of brown cloth pants and an off-white long sleeved blouse. After tucking in the blouse, she put on a dark brown vest with many pockets. She looked in the mirror and applied a minimal amount of eye makeup to emphasize her dark green eyes. Pink lip color finished the look. She may be a pilot, but she was also decidedly female.

She'd been looking forward to the job since the meeting with General Frey and Prince Jory, but having to go around Startia made her nervous. The price on her head from the group she'd been in when she was younger made going anywhere near the planet a risk. She wasn't really looking for trouble to happen on the trip, didn't expect it to happen, but she'd rather deal with the pirates than anything coming from Startia.

She went into her weapons room to see what she might need. She would take her blaster, of course. As a former member of and current contractor to the RPF, they allowed her to keep her blaster. She also picked up her knife. Not an ordinary knife, it had been specially made for Evalycer. The blade, about twenty centimeters long, curved with points at each end. The handle connected to each end of the blade, much like the old brass knuckles gangsters used back on Earth. It allowed her to swing her arm to make her cut, or to stab her opponent without using much force.

Evalycer put both weapons on her belt, and strapped it on around her waist, sitting low just above her hips. After she tied the string of the holster around her right leg to keep it secure, she pulled her straight hair back into a ponytail and grabbed her jacket off a chair. She went out to her vehicle and drove toward the base.

Chapter Six

There was much activity at the base regarding the shipments starting that day. Mechanics had already gone over the ship that Evalycer would be piloting, and Jory and Tobias were going over their ship themselves.

"Do you think we'll have any trouble with this shipment?" Tobias asked as he checked the engine compartments.

"I doubt we will with the first one," Jory said. "They may not know what to expect and scope it out first." He made sure all the connections in the engine were secure.

"I'm hoping for a little excitement," Evalycer said from behind them.

Jory jumped, nearly hitting his head on the engine. He turned around. "Why?" he asked.

"Make this more interesting," she said with a shrug.

"Oh, yeah, I forgot, your last contract was boring," Jory said.

"Seriously, though, I just hope nothing goes wrong," Evalycer said.

Jory looked at her weapons belt and noticed the knife. "That's a serious weapon, there," he said.

Evalycer took it off her belt and handed it to Jory so he could have a closer look.

"One of a kind," she said.

Once in his hand, the knife felt lighter than it looked.

"Very nice," he said, admiring the craftsmanship. "Have you ever used it?"

"A couple times," she said immodestly. "Saved my ass a few times, actually."

"Kill anyone?" Tobias asked.

"Once. I had to protect my honor," she said with mock innocence, splaying her hand on her chest. "He said I wouldn't use it in a fight, that it was just to scare people, so I challenged him to a duel. He doubted my skills, and I got the last laugh."

"General Frey said you were the right person for this job, and I think I agree with him," Jory said, smiling, as he handed the knife back to her. "Glad you're on our side. Maryllia speaks very highly of you."

Evalycer secured the knife back onto her belt. "I'm going to go check on my ship and get the invoice from the general. When do we leave?"

"Oh-nine-hundred."

Evalycer checked her watch. "Okay, I'll see you then." She set off across the hangar bay to her ship.

"Can her ego fit into the ship?" Tobias asked.

Jory laughed. "She's interesting, that's for sure," he said.

An hour later, Maryllia had joined Jory and Tobias at the base.

"Are we ready?" she asked.

"Yeah," said Jory. "We'll leave here in a few minutes."

They walked across the hangar bay to General Frey's office. The general and Evalycer were going over the invoice. He looked up when he saw the group approach.

"Everything set?" General Frey asked.

"We're ready to go," said Jory.

A young man who hardly looked old enough to be on base strode up to them. "Hey, Lees, I replaced the LED in the console and the ship's ready to go," he said.

"Good," she replied, exiting out of the invoice program on the tablet. "We're finished here. General Frey, Major Vance, Captain Kelly, Lieutenant Vance, this is my co-pilot, Aiden Beckett."

"Nice to meet all of you," Aiden said, shaking hands with them.

"Lieutenant Vance will be riding with us on the ship. Major Vance and Captain Kelly will be our escort along with Captain Fletcher and Lieutenant Yates."

"Sounds good," said Aiden.

"I've got a couple more crew members coming in, too, to help run the ship and handle any weapons, just in case," she told Jory.

"I'd like to speak with them before we leave," Maryllia said. "I've also added a few more weapons onboard."

They made their way to their respective ships, where two other men waited for Evalycer. After the introductions, Evalycer told them that after herself, Maryllia was in charge on her ship and her orders should be followed without question. Evalycer followed Maryllia to the weapons station where Maryllia, as head of security on these trips, made sure the men knew how to use all the weapons.

Evalycer walked into the cargo hold where the Elixir had been loaded earlier that morning. She shuffled around the hold to check the bindings on the crates to make sure the cargo wouldn't shift around as they flew. She double checked the invoice to the cargo and saw that everything matched.

She turned off the tablet and slid it into the holder on the wall as she went into the cockpit and slipped on her headset as she sat in the pilot's seat. The ship, *Silver Reign*, wasn't Evalycer's own ship, but she had flown it before and knew its capabilities. She flipped the switches to the power and lights came up on the console, indicating the engines and communications were coming online. As she waited for the ship's engines to come up, Evalycer spoke into the mic.

"This is the *Silver Reign*, requesting permission to depart," she said.

"Permission granted," came the response from Central Command on the base.

"Good luck," said General Frey over the radio. "And be careful."

"We will," said Evalycer. With the engines now online, the *Silver Reign* slowly lifted off and moved forward through the hangar bay. On her monitor she saw Tyrian One and Tyrian Five follow her through the hangar and were soon in the air.

***

As they neared Startia, they had to cut to sub-light engines. They would go around Startia, then once through the asteroid belt, it wasn't much further to Foridian with the sub-light engines.

They brought the ships back to sub-light speed to make the turn toward Startia. Jory noticed the Silver Reign started to take a wider berth of the planet.

"Tyrian One to Silver Reign," Jory said into the mic.

"Go ahead," came Evalycer's voice.

"Why are you flying so far out around the planet?"

"Just taking in the view," she replied.

Jory looked at the planet. The seas on Startia were a brilliant teal color. Combined with the reds and yellows of the vegetation, it did make an attractive view.

"You aren't kidding," Jory said.

"I thought you might like that," Evalycer said.

***

The view notwithstanding, Evalycer definitely wanted to put some distance between her ship and the planet.

Maryllia came up to the cockpit. "Wow, that is beautiful," she breathed.

"I take it you've never been to Startia?" Evalycer asked.

"I think I was there once as a child," Maryllia said. "Our parents had some business there and we went with them because we were so small. I don't remember anything about it."

Good, Evalycer thought. To Maryllia, she said, "I've flown past it a few times in my travels. It is a great view." *With a lousy government.*

Evalycer nudged the thruster forward slightly to get a little more speed. She hoped that Jory didn't notice. She wanted out of that area as fast as possible.

As they came around Startia, they could see Ganta Zay in the distance. Ganta Zay was a reddish-brown, Class 5 planet, on the outermost edge of the Monta Nesta System, bordering the Foridian System. It was much smaller than the other planets, and there was a wispy brown haze surrounding the planet. It had three moons and one small sun.

"Doesn't look very habitable," Jory said.

"People who live there wear face masks outside so they don't breathe in the filthy air," Evalycer came back.

It took an hour to get to the Foridian System. An asteroid belt surrounded the outskirts of the system. Once their ship got within a few hundred meters of the belt, Evalycer contacted the security outpost so they could be escorted through the safest route through the asteroids. The security ship engaged a tractor beam to keep the ship close, and they also secured a shield around both ships, to protect it from any stray asteroids that may come flying by. Jory and Fletcher maneuvered through the belt without help in the smaller fighter ships. Once on the other side of the asteroid belt, the security team disengaged the beam and shield and left the ships. It would be another hour before they reached Foridian.

Snow covered hills came into view as the spacecrafts descended into Foridian's atmosphere. Coniferous trees surrounded lakes and streams on the planet. The governor's spaceport was in a valley with little snow. Green vines made their way up the side of the spaceport. Evalycer requested permission to land. Permission was granted and the *Silver Reign* and the fighter ships landed safely. Malin Garrick greeted them as they disembarked their ships.

"Any trouble getting here?" asked Garrick.

"Nope," Evalycer said. "The route through the asteroids was interesting."

Garrick laughed. "That's about as exciting as it gets, I'm afraid."

Garrick summoned his crew to the ship to begin unloading the Elixir crates while the team went into the lounge to rest and get a bite to eat before they had to leave to go back home.

"You certainly have a beautiful planet," Jory said as Garrick finished checking the invoice.

"Thank you," Garrick said. "In another month, the snow will be gone and it will start to get much warmer. The flowers will start to bloom on the hills and it will look blue and yellow from the distance."

"I look forward to seeing that," Maryllia said.

Once the shipment was unloaded, the crew was back in the air for the trip back to Darantha.

Chapter Seven

The Elixir facilities on both Caledonia and Esray started producing the Elixir again. After several quality checks, they were deemed fully operational. That eased the strain on the Darantha and Ornocto facilities somewhat. Esray helped with the Elixir routes to Yarnell, while Caledonia sent shipments to Foridian.

Over the next two weeks, the trips to and from Foridian were completely uneventful. They had a few tense moments once past the asteroids, as it looked like activity picked up around Ganta Zay, but nothing ever happened, and they cut down the escort to just Jory's ship. Evalycer started to be unconcerned each time they made the trip, but Jory kept on his guard. It seemed too easy, too uncomplicated. Ganta Zay had to know these shipments were passing through their area, and they had threatened to get the Elixir however they could.

Maybe Jory was putting too much stock into thinking the pirates wanted the Elixir for themselves. Experience had taught him to not trust anything, however, no matter how uncomplicated things seemed.

With the next run to Foridian coming up in the next couple of days, Evalycer approached Jory and Tobias as they worked in the control center.

"I really don't think I need an escort anymore," she announced. "We can do this on our own."

"I don't think so," Jory told her, unsmiling. "Just because nothing has happened doesn't mean that it won't. I think General Frey would agree with me."

"I can take care of myself. The ship's got weapon capabilities."

"But you can't maneuver that monstrosity like you can a fighter. I know you're more than capable of handling yourself out there. Too many people are depending on these shipments and I just don't think you should go it alone."

Evalycer stormed off toward the general's office. Jory sighed, and followed a moment later.

Jory could hear Evalycer's voice as he approached the general's office. He knocked loudly on the door to be heard over her ranting. He was beckoned in.

"Lieutenant Nicholls just informed me that she'd like to do this route without an escort," the general started.

"That's what she said to me, as well," Jory replied. "I told her I didn't think it was a good idea."

"I agree," General Frey stated. Jory smiled smugly.

"I don't need protecting!" she shouted.

"Yes, we heard you," Jory said. "Everyone heard you."

"Look, it's only been three weeks since we started this trade route. If nothing happens in the next two weeks, you can go on your own." General Frey looked at her. "Okay?"

"Fine," she said tersely, turned and stomped off toward the hangar bay.

"She's a feisty one," Jory said, watching her leave.

"Yes she is," said the general. "But she's good at what she does."

***

Evalycer was furious. How was she going to ditch the escort so she could go the way *she* wanted to go, which was not around Startia. Every time they went around the planet, she tried to get just a little further away from the planet. Luckily Jory hadn't noticed, but it was only a matter of time before he either realized what was going on, or the faction on Startia found out it was her making the runs past the planet. She'd rather deal with Jory and the general or even the pirates over what the faction would do to her.

If the faction found Evalycer, if they didn't destroy her ship on sight, they'd take her in and probably torture her before killing her. Her betrayal had saved people on Startia, but had thwarted the faction's plans. They were forced underground after that, and Evalycer spent a few months on Monta Nesta to get them off her trail before heading to her home world of Ennek, then Darantha.

Her anxiety rose every time they flew past Startia, but Evalycer was able to hide it from Maryllia. As an interrogator, Evalycer had learned to hide all of her thoughts so no one could use anything against her while doing her job. As good as Maryllia was at peeling away walls to find thoughts in one's mind, Evalycer was that good at hiding them.

**

Two days later, the crew met back at the base to load the shipment for their weekly trip to Foridian. Maryllia came up to Jory, who was checking over his engines. "What did you do to make Evalycer so upset?" she asked.

"She's still upset?" Jory asked. "General Frey and I told her she still needs an escort on these runs," he said. "It wasn't just me that upset her."

Maryllia softened her stance. "Yeah, she likes to do things on her own, not rely on anyone else."

"Well, she's going to have to rely on all of us for at least the next couple of weeks." He told her what General Frey had said.

"That's the smart move," Maryllia agreed.

Once Jory finished with the engines, he and Tobias grabbed something to eat from the cafeteria for the trip, then walked back to their ship. Jory and Tobias put on their headsets as they got into their seats. After going through their pre-flight checklist, they were good to go.

"Tyrian One, ready to go," Jory said into the headset.

"*Silver Reign* ready," came Evalycer's voice through the headset.

"Permission to take off," said General Frey. "Be careful."

"Always, sir," said Jory. He watched as the *Silver Reign* took off, then he and Tobias took off.

An hour into the trip, Jory's ship developed a shudder as he turned the ship to the right. Tobias had just checked the engines, so didn't understand why it wasn't working properly.

"Any ideas?" he asked Tobias. Tobias knew the engines inside and out.

"No," Tobias said, thinking. "I've never felt a ship do that before."

Jory tested it again, turning the ship slightly to the right. It did it again.

"We really can't be flying like this without knowing what's wrong," Tobias said.

"Yeah, I know." He contacted Evalycer. "*Silver Reign*, this is Tyrian One."

"Go ahead," Evalycer replied.

"We've developed some sort of engine problem. We need to find the nearest spaceport and check this out."

"Copy that."

"That means that *you* also have to pull in with us until we can fix this."

"No can do," said Evalycer. "I have a reputation for making my shipments on time. I'm not going to 'pull in' while you figure out what's wrong."

Jory fumed. He turned off his headset to speak to Tobias. "You don't think she did this on purpose, do you?"

"I wouldn't put it past her," Tobias said.

"She better not have sabotaged the ship."

He flipped his headset back on. "*Silver Reign*, I order you to land with us on the nearest planet."

"Technically, I'm not in the RPF anymore," she replied calmly. "I may have held the rank of Lieutenant, but I'm just a pilot-for-hire now. I don't have to follow your orders. I'll see you on Foridian in a few hours."

***

Evalycer smiled smugly as she turned off the headset. She turned her head and winked at Aiden. Maryllia came up behind her.

"What's going on?" she asked.

"Tyrian One has some sort of engine problem," Evalycer told her. "They're going to go to the nearest spaceport to fix it while we continue on to Foridian."

"Is that a good idea?" Maryllia asked. "I know we haven't had any problems going through the Foridian System, but why tempt fate?"

"I think we'll be fine. We've got laser cannons on this ship. Aiden is a pretty good shot, and I know you can hold your own on a cannon."

Maryllia pressed her lips firmly together. Evalycer could see Maryllia wanted to say something, but held back on saying it.

Evalycer had to do some quick thinking. Should she bypass Startia and just go straight to Foridian, flying between Startia and Ganta Zay, or go around Startia as usual, without the escort? At least with the escort, and who the escort was, she'd have a better chance of not getting taken in. How much influence would Maryllia have as a member of the royal family? Either way she went she could be putting a member of the royal family at risk.

Aiden knew her predicament, so if she decided to go between the two planets, she knew he wouldn't say anything. She couldn't risk it—she'd fly between them and take her chances with the pirates.

Instead of turning toward Startia, Evalycer kept on the direct course to Foridian. Aiden didn't say anything, and she hoped Maryllia wouldn't notice until they were well past Startia.

As the *Silver Reign* drew near the sector, Maryllia joined them in the cockpit.

"Why aren't we going around Startia?" Maryllia asked.

"I'm taking the more direct route this time," Evalycer said.

"This is not a good idea, Evalycer," Maryllia said. "We have no protection if anything happens."

"Nothing is going to happen to us. They don't even know we're out here."

They drew near the asteroid belt and signaled the security outpost to take them through. Once through, they all used their abilities to sense any danger that may lie ahead. None of them sensed anything out of the ordinary, but Maryllia was still concerned.

"How much longer until we're out of range of Ganta Zay?" she asked.

"We should be out of range in about ten minutes," Evalycer said. "We'll use our sensors to monitor as well as our abilities, but we should pretty much be home-free."

Maryllia sat in one of the compartments in the ship to have a quiet place to use her mind-reading ability to try and sense everything going on around them. That was one reason she was on the ship, to make sure no one had any intentions of taking the ship or its cargo. Finding it hard to read anything from Ganta Zay, she switched to seeing into the future. She calmed her mind and closed her eyes, focusing on the future. She didn't see anything happening to them as they flew.

Once they were some distance from Ganta Zay, Maryllia opened her eyes again and went back to the cockpit.

"Anything?" Evalycer asked.

"It looks all clear the rest of the way," Maryllia told her.

"Good. Maybe after this we can take this route without the escort."

"You'll probably have a fight on your hands with Jory," Maryllia said. "I don't think he'll be too happy about that, even after this successful run."

***

Jory and Tobias landed their ship on Jenubri, one of the outermost planets in the Darantha System. They found a spaceport quickly using their onboard computer, and landed safely.

Tobias opened the right engine compartment to find out what happened. He looked inside and saw nothing wrong. Jory held a light into the compartment so Tobias could see further in, loosening bolts and moving components out of the way to get back into the engine.

"Right...there!" Tobias said. He pulled out a metal shard, about seven centimeters long, which had been wedged into the engine.

"How the hell did that get in there?" Tobias asked.

"Did we leave the ship unattended at any time?" Jory asked.

"You know we did, while we went to the cafeteria," Tobias said.

"But Evalycer was there the entire time," Jory said. "She was with the foreman, going over the invoice."

They put the engine back together and put the cover back on the compartment. Jory and Tobias got back into their fighter and tested the engines. They seemed okay, but they couldn't be positive until they flew. They took off and once out of gravitational range, Jory performed a series of maneuvers to test the engines. The shudder was gone.

"I've got a few things to say to Evalycer Nicholls once we get to Foridian," Jory said.

They flew around Startia and got to the asteroid field. They contacted the security outpost there to let them know it was just them. Security let them go without an escort.

After passing through the belt, two other ships joined them. They flew around the fighter ship, but didn't fire upon it. Jory and Tobias had to change course several times as they tried to escape the moving blockade. The other ships left quickly after a few more moments of circling the small fighter.

"I wonder what that was all about," Tobias said.

"I wonder if the *Silver Reign* came across the same welcome," Jory replied, worried that something might have happened to the cargo ship. They went light speed again, and were soon reunited with Evalycer, Maryllia, and her crew on Foridian.

***

"Did everything go okay on the trip?" Jory asked over lunch while they waited for the workers to unload the shipment.

"Everything was fine," Maryllia said. "We took a different route, though."

"What do you mean?"

"Instead of going around Startia, we took the direct route to Foridian, past Ganta Zay."

"Are you kidding me?" Jory said, his voice rising.

"Why?"

"We had a little bit of resistance on our way past Ganta Zay," he said.

"What happened?"

Jory told her about the ships flying around them.

"They didn't fire on you?" Evalycer asked, walking up to them.

"No, which was strange. It was like they were just trying to annoy us," Tobias said.

"Or checking us out," Jory said, more to himself than the others.

"What?" Maryllia asked.

"I wonder if they were trying to check us out, see what our capabilities were on the ship," Jory replied. "With you flying past them instead of the regular route, you may have alerted them to our presence."

"So much for hoping to not have an escort," Evalycer said, irritated.

"I didn't read anything on anyone as we passed through the area," Maryllia said. "They were too far away. Even I can't read minds further away than a hundred kilometers."

"I've got some questions for you," Jory said, rounding on Evalycer.

"Why? What'd I do?" she asked, throwing her hands wide.

"Our engine trouble was a metal shard about seven centimeters long, wedged pretty far back into the engine compartment," Tobias answered.

"Well, I don't know anything about the engines on your fighter," she said.

"No? Well, maybe Aiden does." Jory shifted his stance. "Maybe we should have a talk with him about this."

"Maybe we should," she said, and the four of them walked over to where Aiden was helping to unload the crates.

"Hey," Aiden said, wiping the sweat off his forehead with the back of his hand. "You made it."

"Did you do anything to their engines today?" Evalycer barked.

"Why do you ask?"

"Because they found a metal piece in their engines, which is what caused them to have to land on Jenubri."

"Everyone okay?" Aiden asked, looking concerned.

"Yes," said Jory. "But since we had to land, that left the *Silver Reign* unattended. Anything could have happened to you."

"But it didn't, did it? And you both made it okay."

"Barely. We had company on our way past Ganta Zay. Just a patrol checking us out, but who knows what could have happened."

"I don't know why you think I'd do something like that," Aiden said, glancing first at Jory, then at Evalycer.

"Because I think you'd do anything for Evalycer, to help her get what she wants," Jory said, stepping closer to Aiden to get his point across.

Aiden didn't back away. He looked Jory in the eyes, not saying a word. Jory used his mind-reading ability to try to get the truth out of Aiden. He didn't have to do it for long. Aiden wasn't ready for it and had no defense. Jory backed away.

"You *did* do it," Jory said.

"How did you…" Aiden started.

"For fuck's sake," Evalycer said. "He's a mind-reader, Aiden! Of course he'd figure it out."

"Language," Jory smirked.

"You're one to talk," Evalycer said shortly, then turned back to Aiden. "Come with me." Evalycer pulled Aiden over to the side of the hanger.

Jory pretended to not pay attention, but he could hear Evalycer's voice carry over the noise of the bay.

"What were you thinking? Yes, I wanted to do this run without an escort, but not at the expense of potentially hurting someone."

"I'm sorry, Lees. I wasn't thinking straight, I guess."

"Don't make me have to replace you on these runs, Aiden," Evalycer told him firmly. "You're a good co-pilot, but I will replace you if you do anything like this again. Don't ruin my reputation."

"Yes, ma'am," Aiden said. He turned and walked back to where the crates were unloaded.

Evalycer came up to the group again. "I'm truly sorry that happened," she said to Jory, her tone softening. "I hope you didn't think that *I'd* sabotaged your engines."

"The thought had crossed my mind," Jory said. "Only because of how strongly you argued to do the run yourself."

"As much as I want to do this myself, I wouldn't commit treason to do it."

"Treason?"

"Endanger anyone from the royal family?"

"Oh, yeah," Jory said, smiling sheepishly. "I sometimes forget I'm more than just part of the RPF."

On the way back to Darantha, taking the regular route back, everyone was on a heightened sense of alert as they approached the asteroid belt now that they knew that Ganta Zay was aware of them passing through the sector. Evalycer and Aiden were silent as they concentrated on piloting the ship through the sector and around Startia, though Aiden jumped at every little noise from the ship. Maryllia used her abilities to see ahead to make sure they'd remain safe. They returned to Darantha unscathed.

Chapter Eight

Keedu waited in the hangar for his pilots to return. He wanted to know everything about Darantha's fighters and their pilots. He had to know what he was dealing with if he was going to get the Elixir his way. Well, not necessarily his way, but the only way he *could* get it now. He paced anxiously and nearly ran to the pilots as they came in to land.

"Any trouble reading their weaponry?" he asked.

"No sir," the pilot said, handing him the small drive with the information on it. "It should give you everything you need to know, including who is on the ships."

Keedu smiled. "Excellent," he said. "If what's on here proves to be useful, you will be rewarded."

"Thank you, sir," the pilot said.

Keedu went to the elevator to go up to his office eight floors up. The lights came on automatically as he entered the room. He sat at his desk and jammed the drive into the computer portal and brought up the readings. Keedu scrolled through everything quickly, then started at the beginning again, more slowly this time. He pressed a button on his desk and asked Sayzan to come in.

"What do you need?" Sayzan asked as he stood in the doorway.

"Come look at this," Keedu said. Sayzan walked over to view the computer. "This is everything we need to know about the delivery of the Elixir to Foridian."

Sayzan looked over the information. "This will help us with our attacks."

Keedu sat back in his chair, staring at the screen. "We have a lot to plan to pull this off."

***

Back on Darantha, General Frey called the crew into his office for a debriefing.

"What happened out there?" he asked. "How did those fighters know we were flying through there?"

"They do send out patrols every so often," Jory said. "But I believe this time it was because the *Silver Reign* took the straight shot to Foridian instead of going around Startia to put distance between themselves and Ganta Zay."

General Frey turned to Evalycer. "Care to explain why you put everyone in jeopardy?"

Evalycer shifted nervously in her chair. "Well, sir, I didn't think that going around Startia was serving any purpose. The Gantians monitor the entire sector, so either way we go, they could eventually find us."

"Why make it easier for them to do so? You put a lot of people at risk by going that direction."

"My sister being one of them," Jory said. "If you can't follow orders, we'll need to replace you."

Evalycer frowned. She took a deep breath before saying, "I can follow orders."

"Then stay on the planned course," Jory said firmly.

"Yes, sir," Evalycer said, mocking a salute toward Jory.

"I think we'll add Tyrian Five back as an escort next week," General Frey said. "If the Gantians are going to start flying into that sector, we'll need the added protection."

"I think that's a smart move," Jory said, shooting a look at Evalycer, who rolled her eyes.

***

"Hey, Lees," Aiden said as he and Evalycer walked toward the hangar bay. Evalycer stopped and turned toward him. "Why don't you just tell them why you can't go past Startia?"

"Absolutely not," Evalycer said. "That needs to stay in the past."

"I'm pretty sure General Frey would understand…"

"No!" she snapped. "I'll figure out another way to get around the planet."

"You said you didn't want to commit treason, but isn't that what you're doing by not telling them what's going on?"

"Dammit," she said under her breath. Aiden was right. But how could she avoid that without telling them? "I need some time to figure this out."

Evalycer got into her rover and sped away from the base. Instead of driving home, though, she drove to a cantina a few miles outside of the city center. She'd been to this cantina before; with several dark corners to hide in, she liked to come here to do her thinking.

She stopped to get her drink of Ennek scotch from the bartender, then ambled over to her favorite corner. Seated with her back to the wall, she could see everything in the cantina. She didn't expect anything to happen, she just wanted to think and not be surprised by anything.

She sipped her drink. How was she going to work this out? She had hoped that this would never come out, but now it looked like she'd have to come clean. She couldn't put Prince Jory and Princess Maryllia in danger. Aiden knew what had happened and knew the risks, but she was putting him in danger, too, by knowingly committing treason. He'd do anything for her and keep his mouth shut. She knew he looked up to her, like the big sister he never had.

Evalycer slammed back her drink, and motioned to a server for another one. Her integrity and work ethic made it hard for her to keep this quiet. She knew that Jory needed to know the story if she wanted to keep doing these deliveries for the RPF. She sighed, and pulled out her communicator.

***

After the meeting, Jory watched Tobias work out with the Virtual Opponent. Tobias had called up the program that would increase its strength as Tobias progressed. Although the VO was holographic, it could pack a punch. Tobias got hit a few times, which made him work harder.

As Jory watched, his com buzzed. He pulled it off his belt and looked at the message.

"Hey, I gotta go," Jory shouted over the noise of Tobias's workout.

"Pause program," Tobias said. The VO stopped mid-punch. "What's up?"

"Lieutenant Nicholls wants to see me," Jory said, putting the com back on his belt.

"I'll get cleaned up and go with you," Tobias said.

Jory shook his head. "She wants me to come by myself."

"That doesn't sound good."

"No, it doesn't." Jory turned to leave with a wave to Tobias.

Jory wasn't familiar with the part of the city where Evalycer told him to meet her. He finally found the place. It was well back from the street, surrounded by a high fence. He went inside. The place was dark, so it took a few moments for his eyes to adjust to the dimness. When he could finally see somewhat, he looked over the customers and finally spotted Evalycer's blonde hair back in a corner. He made his way around the tables and customers to the table and said down. A server came over and asked Jory for his order.

***

65

"What did you need to see me about?" Jory asked. Despite the cantina being fairly busy, it was also fairly quiet. Music played in the background, but in Evalycer's corner, it was more subdued.

"I owe you an explanation," Evalycer started. The server brought Jory's drink.

"Yes, you do," Jory said.

Evalycer took a deep breath and blew it out slowly. "Eight years ago, I lived on Startia," she began. "After I graduated from the Academy there, I joined this group of people who wanted to change the government. You know that the government there at the time was very corrupt."

"Yes," Jory said. "They wanted the best and brightest from the Academy to work for them."

"It wasn't that they wanted it, it was required. Enter yours truly, one of the best mind-readers in her class." She took a drink from her glass. "I of course wanted no part in the government. What they wanted were spies to make sure people were staying in line. I wasn't going to do it, so I joined this faction of renegades. We were young and so smart, or so we thought." Evalycer laughed. "Yeah, so smart. We were going to take down the whole government.

"Our plan was to sneak into the government offices and take the officials hostage until our demands were met, which was for Governor Atouu to step down," she said. "He just wanted money and power. He didn't care about his people," she said angrily, taking a sip of her scotch.

"I remember hearing some of this," Jory said. "My parents sent me to Caledonia for a conference for young leaders and they talked about Atouu's government."

"As time went on, things started to take a darker turn. I started reading the leaders minds and found out they weren't just planning on taking hostages, they were going to kill Atouu."

Evalycer paused for a few moments, thinking about that time. She was glad that Jory let her sit in her silence. A tear ran down her cheek. She wiped it away quickly before Jory could see it, pretending to scratch her cheek instead.

"That didn't sit well with me. I was in that group to make changes, not kill people. I knew I had to do something. I read their minds every chance I got—that's how I became so good at finding out what people are hiding. The leaders were really excited about killing Atouu. Once I had enough information, I went to Atouu's offices and told them what was going to happen. At first they didn't believe me, but after I submitted to a mind probe, they knew I was telling the truth. Though it can hide the truth, the mind doesn't lie."

Evalycer looked at Jory, whose wide-eyed expression told her he was surprised.

"Even though you hated his government, you still protected him," Jory stated.

"Yes," Evalycer said. "I didn't mind taking him down and scaring him, but I wasn't into killing. With the information I gave them, they moved Atouu to another location, and all we ended up doing was blowing up the offices, which I ended up not taking part of. I was ill the night they did it.

"Once they found out I was the one to tip off Atouu, the leaders came after me. I left Startia and went to Monta Nesta for about six standard months, then to Ennek. I then came here and joined the RPF, mostly to hide from the faction. They put a price on my head, and it wasn't to just capture me, but to kill me."

"And if you go near Startia, they will probably do other things to you before killing you," Jory said, understanding her dilemma.

Evalycer nodded. She felt slightly relieved, but now she had new worries. Would she be dismissed from this assignment? Would she be charged with treason? She looked at Jory, who seemed to be pondering the same things as she.

Jory stared into the untouched drink in his hands. After a time, he finally spoke. "I have to tell General Frey about all this," he said slowly.

Evalycer leaned her head back, looking up at the ceiling, mouth open, sighing deeply. *My business and life are over.*

"But, I'm going to recommend—insist—that you stay on this job. You're a great pilot and I trust you. The way you laid into Aiden when he sabotaged our ship showed me that you can be trusted, plus Maryllia speaks highly of you, and I trust my sister implicitly. What you've told me will not go any further than Frey."

"You're not going to tell your sister or Captain Kelly?"

"No. I'll only tell them what they need to know and it was a good enough reason for me."

Feeling the weight of all this lifting off her shoulders, she laughed out loud. "Great! Oh my God, you don't know what I've been trying to do to avoid Startia on these runs. I wasn't flying so far around the planet for the view. I didn't want them to detect me on the ship."

"I think the sooner we tell General Frey, the better," Jory said.

Evalycer finished her drink. "You're right," she said. "I'll meet you at the base in an hour."

"See you then," Jory said, and he left the cantina.

Chapter Nine

Jory arrived back at the base and went to his office. Tobias sat at his desk taking care of some correspondence.

"How'd it go?" Tobias asked, looking up from his computer.

"It went well," Jory said, sitting down at his desk.

"What happened?"

"I can't tell you everything," Jory said. "I *can* tell you that her integrity is unmatched. We can trust her."

Tobias looked confused, but didn't say anything further. Jory turned to work at his computer until he got a message that Evalycer was looking for him.

"I'll be back," Jory said, and he left to go meet with General Frey and Evalycer.

After telling the story to General Frey, Evalycer and Jory waited for his comments.

"I'm not happy about this," Frey said, leaning back in his chair, his jaw muscles tensing. "You put a lot of people in danger. Major Vance has every right to be upset about this."

"Yes, sir," Evalycer said.

General Frey said nothing, much like Jory had done when Evalycer gave him her story. He stood up and paced the floor, looking much taller than his two meters. Jory and Evalycer looked at each other, not knowing what to expect. Finally Frey turned around. "I trust Major Vance's judgement. You will remain on this assignment. However, there will be consequences that we'll discuss later."

Evalycer visibly relaxed. "Yes, sir."

"Are we in agreement that no one else needs to know about this?" Jory asked cautiously.

Even though General Frey had spoken calmly, Jory could see he was upset. Frey's jaw was set and his mouth a firm line.

"We do not need to tell anyone else about this," Frey said. "Major Vance, you can tell Lieutenant Vance and Captain Kelly as much as they need to know about the decision to not fly past Startia."

"Yes, sir," Jory said, smiling at Evalycer.

"I will be watching you, Lieutenant," Frey said to Evalycer. "Don't make me regret this decision."

"I won't, sir. Thank you, sir," Evalycer said, this time taking no umbrage at the rank misuse.

Jory and Evalycer stood, Jory nodding respectfully at General Frey before they both left the office.

Evalycer cleared her throat. "Um, thanks for everything," she said. With more sincerity, she added. "I appreciate what you're doing for me."

"Like Frey, don't make me regret it."

Evalycer winked. "I won't."

The following week the crew got ready for their next run. This would be a longer trip than usual. Samara would join them this time to see how the Foridians were handling the effects of the Elixir.

"I wish you didn't have to go on this trip," Jory said as he and Samara packed their bags for the trip. "It makes me uneasy."

"I trust you and Tobias to keep all of us safe," Samara replied, closing her bag.

"Tyrian Five will be with us on this trip. The *Silver Reign* has weapons, but I'm not sure how we'd do against more than two or three fighters." Jory pulled out his blaster. "Here, I'm going to show you how to fire this thing," he told her.

"Do you really think I'll have to use one?"

"Hopefully, you won't, but I want you to know how, just in case."

Jory showed her all the parts to the blaster, how to take the safety off, and how to hold it.

"It does have a stun feature, which I never use," he said, showing her the switch. "I'm shooting to kill. If you don't feel comfortable killing, use stun. It will disable someone for about a minute, allowing you to get away." As Samara looked over the weapon, Jory continued. "I want to show you how to use the guns on the *Silver Reign* before we go. Maryllia already knows how to use them, but if it came to it, I want you to be able to defend yourself and the ship. I've trained you in hand-to-hand fighting, but you should know how to use weapons, as well."

They arrived early at the base the next morning so Jory could show Samara how to use the weapons on the *Silver Reign*. He saw Evalycer heading over to the ship and he and Samara followed.

"Lieutenant," Jory called to her.

Evalycer stopped and turned around, annoyed. "Oh my God, stop calling me that," she said crossly. "Call me Miss Nicholls if you have to call me something respectful, but I prefer Evalycer, or Lees."

"Fine, Miss Nicholls," Jory said. "I want to show my wife Samara how to use the weapons on board, just in case. Sam, this is Evalycer Nicholls, the pilot of the *Silver Reign*. Miss Nicholls, my wife, Samara."

Samara extended her hand to shake Evalycer's. "Your Highness," Evalycer said, grasping Samara's hand and nodding respectfully. "Happy to meet you."

"So nice to meet you, too," Samara said. "Jory's told me a lot about you."

Evalycer laughed. "Uh-oh. I'm definitely in trouble now."

"He says you're a good pilot with a good work ethic," Samara replied with a smile.

"You're too kind to say what he's really said about me, your Highness," Evalycer said. "But thank you."

"Can we show her how to use the weapons?" Jory asked.

"I don't think she'll ever have to use them, with my crew on board," Evalycer told him.

"I know, but I'd like for her to know, just to be safe."

Evalycer rolled her eyes. "He's so anxious about these trips," she said, but she took them on board and down the corridor to one of the weapons stations. "This is, I think, the less complicated to learn quickly. Have a seat," Evalycer told Samara, forgetting to use any kind of title.

Samara sat in the seat and both Jory and Evalycer showed her how to use the station. It was a straight forward "pull the trigger" type of weapon, but it had to be charged before using it. Samara understood it right away.

"So, *if* it comes to you having to use a weapon," Evalycer said. "This is the one."

"I already showed her how to use a blaster, too," Jory said. "So if anything happens, she's prepared."

"I hate that half the royal family is going to be on this trip," Evalycer said. "Makes me nervous."

"You? Nervous?" Jory said in jest. "I'd never have thought that *you'd* get nervous."

"I do, on occasion," Evalycer replied.

Once Tobias and Maryllia arrived, Jory called everyone to a brief meeting before they left on the trip.

"We will not be flying around Startia anymore," Jory told them. Both Tobias and Maryllia looked taken aback.

"What? Why not?" Maryllia asked.

"The area has been deemed too dangerous for us to travel through anymore, so…"

"More dangerous than flying the direct route with the possibility of the Gantians intercepting us?" Tobias asked.

"Yes," Jory said firmly. "I spoke with General Frey yesterday and it was decided to go the direct route from now on."

No one said anything else. Jory looked at Evalycer, who at least had the good sense to not look self-satisfied. He suspected that he'd hear from both Tobias and Maryllia later on in private, but right now, they had a delivery to make.

Once airborne, they hit light speed on course for the asteroid belt.

"So, why the change?" Tobias asked. "We're more at risk going this route than around Startia. Isn't Startia a peaceful planet?"

"Yes, they are," Jory said. "But there was something brought to my attention yesterday that I had to discuss with General Frey, and it turns out we're being put in danger when we fly past Startia."

"Did Nicholls know about this?"

"Yes, but I can't go into any details right now."

Tobias didn't ask any more questions. The ships came up on the asteroid belt. Jory contacted the security post to escort the *Silver Reign* through while his ship and Tyrian Five followed on their own.

Once they got past the asteroid belt, everyone stayed vigilant in keeping an eye out for any ships on their monitors. Everyone used their ability to see into the future, as it would be too difficult to read the minds of the people on Ganta Zay.

***

"Keedu," Sayzan said.

Keedu came to the controller desk. "What is it?"

"We've just spotted the ships from Darantha coming through the asteroid belt," Sayzan said. "They'll hit light speed any moment."

"Send the ships out. Make sure to flood that area with the deactivation beam. Let's let them know that we mean business. We won't hurt them this time, just scare them a little."

***

Maryallia of course was the first to see anything.

"We're going to have company very soon," she said into her headset.

"Dammit," Jory said. "How can they even see us since we're going light speed?"

"I don't know," Maryallia told him. "But they will be here soon."

"Charge up the weapons," Evalycer said.

Maryllia and the other crew members ran to charge the weapons. Samara moved to do the same, but Maryllia stopped her.

"We'll charge your weapon," Maryallia told her. "But I want you to stay put until we absolutely need you, Samara. Buckle yourself into your seat for now."

Samara did as she was told, while Maryllia charged the weapons.

The Silver Reign dropped out of light speed, as did the escort fighters.

"What the hell?" Evalycer exclaimed. "What happened?"

"I don't know," Jory said over the headset. "We've got propulsion only right now."

"Ships coming in," Tobias said.

"Not good," Evalycer said.

Ships came racing in and flew around the Silver Reign and the escorts, but didn't fire on them, just like the previous weeks' incident. Like annoying flies they hung around the ships, sometimes flying at them, only to pull up at the last minute.

As suddenly as they came, they left without harming the ships.

"What the hell was that all about?" Evalycer asked.

"How's Samara?" Jory asked over the radio.

Maryllia looked at Samara. Samara had turned pale and had a solid grip on the edge of her seat.

"A little shaken," Maryllia replied. "But okay."

Evalycer flipped switched and pushed buttons, but the hyper-drive wouldn't come back online. "The hyper-drive is dead," she announced. "But the engines seem okay."

"Us, too," Jory said. "Let's try and coax more speed out of them and get to Foridian."

***

Governor Oxmoor had been alerted to the attack and was waiting at the spaceport to greet them all. Jory ran to the Silver Reign and when the door opened, he ran in and embraced Samara tightly.

"Are you okay?" he whispered into her ear.

"Yes," Samara said, though Jory could still feel her trembling.

Jory pulled back to look at her. "I was so scared when those ships came in, I thought I was going to lose you."

"I was in good hands," she said, smiling nervously.

They followed the crew out the door where Governor Oxmoor waited for them.

"So happy to see all of you in one piece," Governor Oxmoor said, shaking hands with Jory and Tobias and being introduced to Evalycer. "Is everyone all right?"

"Yes," Jory said, squeezing Samara's hand.

Governor Oxmoor led them to a room where they could regroup and get refreshments before conducting business. Jory wanted to make sure Samara really was okay. While the rest of them were used to battles, Samara was not. The closest she'd ever gotten was when Radern had pulled her into a shield position at the base last year. He knew she was a strong woman, but he worried about her.

After Samara assured Jory that she could continue with the meeting, Jory and Samara met with the governor and his representatives while the crates of Elixir were unloaded. They were

75

both happy to learn that the Elixir was being well-tolerated by everyone. Jory had been concerned that people may try to abuse it, take advantage of the effects and crime would go up.

"We've incorporated a few new laws to deter any abuse," Governor Oxmoor said with a smile.

"Sounds like everything in under control," Samara said. "I'd like to visit with your representatives, just to see how they are tolerating the Elixir and their abilities and do some observations."

"I'll have my advisor Malin Garrick set that up for you for later this evening."

"Thank you," Samara said.

Later that evening, after Samara had met with the governor's representatives, Jory and Samara decided to go out for dinner, and asked Maryllia and Tobias if they wanted to join them.

"Yeah, I'd like to check this place out," Maryllia said. "Do some observations of the people, to see how the Elixir is working for them."

"Oh, good," said Samara. "I was thinking of doing the same thing while we're out."

"And you get mad at *me* for working after hours," Jory said with a grin.

"Should we ask Miss Nicholls if she'd like to go, too?" Samara asked.

"I guess that's the polite thing to do," Jory said.

"Don't you like her?" Samara asked.

"I like her well enough," Jory told her. "She just seems detached from everyone, wants to do things her way."

Aa Samara and Maryllia got ready to go, Jory and Tobias walked down the hall to Evalycer's room and Jory knocked. A moment later Evalycer opened the door.

"Hey," Jory started. "The four of us were going out and wondered if you wanted to go with us?" he asked.

Evalycer looked at the both of them, then shook her head. "Nah, I don't want to be a fifth wheel."

Jory considered that for a moment, then laughed. "You won't be a fifth wheel," he told her. "Tobias and my sister are not together."

Tobias looked dumbfounded for a moment, then found his voice. "I'm engaged to someone else, not to Maryllia," he said, smiling.

Evalycer looked relieved. "Give me five minutes and I'll meet you in the lobby."

"See you then," Jory said, and Evalycer closed the door.

Five minutes later, they all met in the lobby, ready to go. "Apparently, this is going to be a work night," Jory said as they walked out the doors on into the flow of foot traffic.

"Why?" Evalycer asked.

"Sam and Maryllia are going to be observing people and their reactions to the Elixir," he said.

They walked along the walkway until they found a restaurant that had a table available. They sat down and the server came to take their drink order.

"A glass of Pelonsa Reserve," Evalycer said when her turn came. At 100-proof, Pelonsa Reserve was illegal in the Darantha System, though it could be obtained by people who knew where to look.

"You certainly are full of surprises," Jory said.

"It's not illegal here," Evalycer said. "So you betcha I'm going to order it."

They looked over the menu as they waited for the drinks. The server brought them a few minutes later, setting Jory's more reserved 20-proof Ennek scotch in front of him.

Jory could see Maryllia and Samara concentrating on the people around them. He did a little observing himself, and found nothing out of the ordinary. Everyone seemed to be tolerating the Elixir as they should. Still a novelty for them, every so often someone would make something fly across the room, but nothing that would suggest that the Elixir was being abused.

Samara and Maryllia compared their findings. They'd come to the same conclusion as Jory, that nothing dishonest was going on. After that, they enjoyed their evening.

Once back at their hotel, they parted ways, going to their rooms while Evalycer went to work on her ship's hyper-drive. They were going back home in the morning and the ship needed all its capabilities.

Chapter Ten

The following week, Samara flew to the Yarnell System to check on the people there while Jory made his run to Foridian. Samara's assistant accompanied her, so Jory felt better about her going without him. Jory didn't need to worry, however, since the Yarnell System was in a more peaceful part of the galaxy. It was a longer trip, though, taking a full day to get there. She would be gone for three days total.

The Foridian crew was ready to make their trip. Jory paced nervously around his ship, hitting his fists on top of each other while he waited for Tobias.

"What's wrong?" Tobias asked as they prepared to board their ship.

"I saw something during my meditation this morning," he said, frowning.

"What was it?"

"It was too quick, but I felt that we were in danger."

"I hate when you have these visions," Tobias said.

"We'll have to make sure that everyone is on alert and staying focused on the trip."

Jory found Evalycer a few minutes later and told her about what he saw.

"Finally, some action," she said excitedly. "I'm assuming it was as we passed Ganta Zay?"

"Not sure, but most likely," Jory said. "We need to be careful."

"Will do," she said, and she gathered her crew together to tell them about this development.

Jory saw Maryllia making her way to the group, but he beckoned her over to him.

"I think it may be a good idea if you stay here," he told her. He told her about the vision.

"I'm not going to not do my job because you say it's too dangerous," she said. "I'm a trained member in the RPF and this is my assignment. I'm not going to back out of it now. Besides, you'll need all the help you can get."

"Stubborn as always," he said, smiling. "Okay, but be careful."

Evalycer checked over her ship and weapons as the crew loaded the shipment onto the *Silver Reign*. She checked everything inside as well.

"I think once we get past the asteroid belt," she started. "We should charge the weapons, just in case."

"Not a bad idea," Jory said. "We shouldn't be detected while going light speed, but you can't be too careful."

They started their journey to Foridian. Once through the asteroid belt, Evalycer had her crew charge their weapons. Jory used his ability to try to see into the future.

"Major Vance," Evalycer said into her headset. "Have you seen anything yet?"

"Negative," Jory replied. "But that doesn't mean we won't."

"Lieutenant Vance is also looking into the future, so maybe she'll be able to see something."

Maryllia came out a few moments later. "We're going to have some company on this trip," she told Jory on the headset and Evalycer in the cockpit.

Tobias saw a couple of ships on the screen heading their way.

"Here they come," Jory said into the headset.

"I've got flaming pie ready for them," Evalycer replied.

The two ships from Ganta Zay came up quickly, followed by two more. All four of the ships flew around Jory's fighter and the *Silver Reign*, trying to nudge the *Silver Reign* toward Ganta Zay.

"If they think that's all it's going to take to make me go off course," Evalycer said. "They better think again."

"Are your weapons covered?" Jory asked.

"Yes," Evalycer told him. "Lieutenant Vance is on one cannon, Xander on the other," indicating her other crew member.

"Good. We're ready, too."

The *Silver Reign* and the fighter stayed on course despite the four ships' best efforts to run them off course and toward Ganta Zay. The ships took turns, it seemed, flying at the cargo ship, but none of them fired on the ships. Jory and Tobias maneuvered around the ships and took a run at some of Ganta Zay's ships as well. Jory used his abilities to see ahead and fly out of the way just in the nick of time, barely missing the fighter ships. Evalycer used her abilities to read the pilots minds to know what they were going to do next to keep her ship out of harm's way. Maryllia read the minds of the pilots to try to figure out what they wanted specifically.

"They definitely want the Elixir," Maryllia said. "They're trying to drive us closer to Ganta Zay so our cargo can be scanned…"

"We're being scanned as we speak," Evalycer said. She picked up the signal from the cargo hold. "I'm sure they want to know how much of the Elixir we have with us. The signal is coming from the planet itself. They have very advanced monitoring capabilities."

"Damn it," Jory said.

"So, it's a good bet they know how much we're carrying," she said.

Just as quickly as they came, the fighters took off as the *Silver Reign* and Jory's fighter were past Ganta Zay and out of scanning range.

"Well, that was fun," Evalycer said sarcastically.

They continued on their course to Foridian. Once there, they told Governor Oxmoor what had happened and what they had found out.

"They want the Elixir, Governor," Jory told him. "No doubt about it. They scanned our cargo, so I'm pretty sure they're planning something."

"I'll have my pilots ready to go next week, in case something does happen and you need back-up," the governor said. "My pilots have been training on using their abilities as they fly, and some of them are very good at it now."

"That will be helpful," said Jory. "Hopefully it won't come to that."

***

Once back on Darantha, Jory told General Frey about the attack.

"Governor Oxmoor will send his troops to help us if we need it," Jory finished.

"Make sure you take him up on his offer," General Frey said. "I know you like to do things on your own, but…"

"I'll be happy to have the help, actually," Jory said.

"Maybe we should send more fighters with you next time," the general said.

"Foridian is closer to Ganta Zay than Darantha is," Jory said. "It would make more economical sense to use their resources than to have even one of ours go with us."

"You're right, as always," the general grinned.

Later that evening, Jory spoke with Samara on Yarnell.

"I'm going to speak with the pilots and make sure that they are on their guard as they come home," he said. "I know that Yarnell is peaceful, but I'm…"

"Just being cautious," Samara finished. "I love you for it. See you in a couple days."

***

"Their weapons are basic," Keedu said into the communicator on the console. "As are the crew. Their weapons can't penetrate the duratatium."

"Good," came the reply. "They will be making the usual run next week. Make sure your tractor beam is ready."

"It will be ready, as will the deactivator."

"I cannot do anything from here to help you," the voice said. "It will look too suspicious."

"We'll have everything under control," Keedu said.

Keedu hit the button to end the communication and sat back in his chair. The Elixir, the infusion that gave people certain powers, would soon be available to him and his crew. He thought about all the ways he could control the people on Ganta Zay as well as take advantage of the ships as they passed through the area. While he didn't know what abilities he'd have, he'd find a way to use them to his benefit. Right now, he had the people controlled by the patrols he sent out to keep everyone in line. He looked forward to learning to use whatever abilities he gained from the Elixir.

Chapter Eleven

Jory finished his meditation and opened his eyes, frowning. He didn't like what he saw for the trip that day. He pulled on his uniform jacket and went to find Evalycer and Tobias. He found Tobias first and told him what he saw.

"Not good," Tobias said.

"I know," Jory replied. "We need to find Evalycer and let her know."

They found her, going over the invoice from a side job she'd done the day before.

"Evalycer, we may have a problem today," Jory said.

"Wait," she said, sitting down. "This is a momentous occasion."

"What the hell?" Jory said, confused.

"You called me by my first name. I had to sit and let it sink in for a moment."

"Oh, for crying out loud," Jory scoffed, rolling his eyes. "Can we get to the business at hand?"

"What's up?" Evalycer asked, standing again.

"I saw something happening today during my meditation."

"You, too?" she asked, surprised. "I saw something as well."

They compared their visions, and concluded the trip to Foridian would be much different than usual.

"Once we get past the asteroid belt, we'll charge weapons and be on alert," Evalycer said. "Your sister will have to put her skills into play today."

"Maryllia's not going today," Jory said. "No way."

"I think she'll tell you differently," Evalycer remarked.

Jory, Tobias, and Evalycer went to the general's office to tell him what they'd seen.

"Make sure you contact Governor Oxmoor as soon as you're getting close to Ganta Zay," General Frey said. "He can send his fighters to help."

"Will do, sir," Jory assured the general. They left the office and Jory saw Maryllia crossing the hanger bay to the ship. He ran up to her, Evalycer following.

"I saw something happening today on the trip," he started.

"Yeah, so did I," Maryllia replied. "We need to be on…"

"You're not going," he said firmly.

"Oh, the hell I'm not, Jory," Maryllia said. "I'm trained to do this. I'm the best you have in seeing the future and mind reading, that's why I'm on this team."

"I'm not going to let you go. I out-rank you."

"You're not going to pull this rank bullshit on me," she warned, using the forbidden word boldly. It surprised Jory that his by-the-rules sister even knew how to use the word. "If this were anyone else, you'd have no problem but because I'm your *sister*, I have to stay here? Not going to happen."

Evalycer stood there, watching the exchange, smirking. "I told you," she said to Jory.

"And you know General Frey would say that same thing," Maryllia said. "You tried this once before, and it didn't work. What made you think it would this time?"

"Okay," Jory relented. "Be careful."

"I always am," she said with a playful punch to Jory's arm.

"'Bullshit'?" he asked with a smirk.

Maryllia smiled sheepishly. "We're out of ear-shot of our superiors, unless *you* say something."

Jory held up his hands in surrender. "Nope, I've got no room to talk."

When the time came to leave, they all returned to the hangar bay to their ships and started their flight to Foridian.

After they got through the asteroid belt, the security team left them to their journey past Ganta Zay.

"Maryllia, Xander," Evalycer started. "Start charging the weapons, please."

"You got it," Maryllia said, and she went down the corridor with Xander to the weapons bay to start charging the laser cannons and other weapons. When Maryllia came back up, Evalycer handed her a headset.

"You should probably have one of these, so you can communicate with us and your brother once we engage the fighters," Evalycer told her.

Maryllia put the headset on and checked that it worked, then went off to meditate and see what would happen as they got closer to Ganta Zay.

"I'm going to contact Governor Oxmoor and have his pilots meet us as we near Ganta Zay," Jory told Evalycer over the radio.

"Copy that," she said.

Governor Oxmoor told Jory that he was sending his fighters now and would only take a few minutes for them to reach the Ganta Zay region.

"Everyone on alert," Jory said into his headset.

"Roger that," Evalycer replied. "Maryllia, get ready."

"Yes, ma'am," came Maryllia's voice through the headset.

As they got closer to Ganta Zay, Aiden spotted four incoming ships from the planet.

"Shields up!" Evalycer said. Aiden hit a button to engage the shields.

The ships from Ganta Zay flew around the *Silver Reign* and Jory's ship, firing at them both. The *Silver Reign* didn't have the maneuverability that Jory's ship had, so Jory flew around to intercept the fighters. Jory knew that the *Silver Reign*'s crew were firing the cannons, hitting their marks but doing little damage.

"What are these things made out of?" Evalycer exclaimed in the headset.

"Have you run a scan on the ships?" Jory asked.

"Not yet," Evalycer said. "Been a little busy. Xander's doing it now."

As they waited for the results, three fighters from Foridian came in, lasers firing. They hit the Gantian ships, but, like Jory and Evalycer, did little damage.

"We have something," Evalycer said. "Duratatium."

"Dura-what?" Jory replied.

"Duratatium."

"I've never heard of that," Jory said. He turned to Tobias. "Have you?"

"No," Tobias said, rolling the ship out of the way of an oncoming ship.

"It's the most durable metal found in this region," said Governor Oxmoor over the com. "It's also quite heavy, which usually makes it impossible to use on ships."

"Looks like they found a way to use it," Evalycer said.

The Gantian ships kept firing at the *Silver Reign*. Not trying to destroy it, but to try to make it turn towards Ganta Zay. Evalycer held her position, although the ship sustained minor damage. Maryllia and Xander returned fire, while the Foridian ships and Jory fired upon the Gantian ships.

Jory and Tobias went after one ship that was doing most of the firing on the *Silver Reign*. They fired on it, and the ship fired back at them, turning to follow them, away from the *Silver Reign*. Jory and Tobias performed maneuvers to escape the blasts of the ship. One of the Foridian fighters came and shot at the ship, but only knocked out one of the firing tubes. The rest of the Foridian fighters successfully drew the Gantian fighters away from the *Silver Reign*. Once they were far past the planet, the Gantian fighters broke off and flew back toward Ganta Zay.

"Should we follow them?" a Foridian pilot asked.

"Negative," Jory said. "I don't think it would be beneficial right now. We should just follow course and get to Foridian as soon as possible."

Jory and the *Silver Reign* followed the Foridian fighters to Foridian. Once they landed, the crew met in the hangar.

"Anyone hurt? Any damage on your ship?" Jory asked Evalycer.

"No injuries," Evalycer started. "They knocked out the ship's thermostat before we got the shields up, so the ride home is going to be a little cold."

"We'll see what we can do to help out," Governor Oxmoor told her, walking up to the group.

"Thanks for your help, Governor," Jory said, shaking Oxmoor's hand.

While the Foridian workers unloaded the Elixir, the crew went to get something to eat in the lounge. Evalycer ordered a shot of Ennek scotch, and promptly downed it in one gulp and ordered another. Jory joined her at the bar.

"You okay?" he asked, concerned.

"Oh, yeah," Evalycer told him. The bartender brought her drink to her. "Cheers!" she said, as she raised her glass and tossed that one back as well. She sighed, and said, "That was crazy up there, wasn't it?"

"Yes, it was," Jory agreed. "Your crew did well up there."

"They did a hell of a job firing at those fighters."

"You did well, too, staying on course through it all."

The bartender had brought her another drink. "Well," she said. "I don't like to be forced into anything. If they want me to fly that way, they'll have to use a tractor beam." She stared at her drink for a moment. "I was kind of nervous up there," she said quietly. She looked sharply at Jory. "Don't you dare tell anyone I said that."

"I won't breathe a word of it," he said, smirking. He placed his hand gently on her forearm. "Come on. We've got a table so we can eat before we go back."

Evalycer picked up her glass and followed Jory to the table where the server was already taking everyone's food order.

As they finished eating, Evalycer got word that they were done unloading the Elixir. They paid for the meals and went back to the hangar.

"Were you able to fix the thermostat on the *Silver Reign*?" Evalycer asked.

"We have it rigged up to keep the compartments semi-warm," the foreman said. "But only use it when it starts getting too cold. Otherwise, it will break down before you get home."

"Thanks," she said, shaking the foreman's hand.

Back on Darantha, Jory and Evalycer reported to General Frey about the incident.

"I believe they are going to keep trying to get the shipment each week," Jory told him.

"Your ship sustained damage?" General Frey asked, turning to Evalycer.

"Yes," she said. "It's being repaired right now. Luckily the thermostat was the only thing damaged in the attack. My crew did an outstanding job keeping the fighters at bay."

"We couldn't penetrate the hulls of their fighters," Jory told the general. "We found out they were made of duratatium. I've never heard of that."

"Back when we had the conference, a few days later, Keedu from Ganta Zay contacted me, wanting to make a deal to get the Elixir, which I told you about."

"Yes, I remember," Jory said.

"They wanted to trade duratatium for the Elixir. I told them we didn't deal with criminals. I didn't know anything about the mineral, but now I wished I'd looked into it a little more." He sat down behind his desk. "We'll need to rethink how we get the shipments there. Next week, fly around Jenubri. It's a longer trip, but it will be safer, and puts you well beyond Startia and Ganta Zay."

"That will make the entire trip take a whole day," Evalycer complained.

"You know what the alternative is. Take it or leave it," the general said, though he knew which she'd choose.

"I'll take it," Evalycer said.

Chapter Twelve

Jory had to be at the base early the next morning. He had a meeting with General Frey and a few of the construction engineers for the Elixir facilities on Foridian and Yarnell. He would most likely be sent to Foridian and possibly Yarnell to check on the progress of the construction there.

He got out of bed without waking Samara. He grabbed something out of the refrigerator to eat on the way to the base, and drank his Elixir as he walked out to his land-rover.

Jory arrived at the base a few minutes later, checked his correspondence before making his way to the general's office for the meeting at 0800.

"Good, we're all here," said General Frey after beckoning Jory into the office.

Jory sat down and General Frey started the meeting. The screens came up and the faces of the foremen from Foridian and Yarnell came into view.

"This is just an informal meeting to see how the construction is going on your planets," General Frey started.

"It's going well on Foridian," said Anze Martell, the foreman of the construction company. "We're on schedule and haven't had any problems."

"We've had a couple of issues," said the foreman from Yarnell, Kyle Elliot. "We've had problems with the building supplies, but we've switched to another supplier and we're almost back on schedule."

"How far behind are you?" Jory asked.

"Only one week. But we're spending an extra hour each day to catch up. We'll be back on track in the next week or so."

"Good," said Frey. "Sounds like you've both got everything under control. Next week, Major Vance will be visiting the sites on Foridian and Yarnell to check on things there."

"Sounds good," Kyle Elliot said. "We'll look forward to it."

Their faces faded from view.

General Frey sat there at his desk, staring at the viewer for a moment before speaking to Jory.

"You know why I send *you* on these visits, don't you?" the general finally said.

"Sir?" Jory said, confused.

"I always send you on these trips because of your ability to read people's minds. You're not as good as your sister, but pretty damn close."

"Thank you, sir. I never questioned…"

"I know you haven't. I also send you because of who you are. They will be more forthcoming to you than anyone else. At least, I hope they are."

"I've never had a problem with anyone not telling me the truth," Jory chuckled.

"And you proved that I can trust you to do any assignment I give you, after that mission last year."

"Don't remind me." Jory had tried to push that whole mission out of his mind once it was over.

"I'll have one of the foremen from our facility as well as an engineer go with you when you visit Foridian and Yarnell. The sooner we can get these facilities up and running, the sooner we can stop making these trips to Foridian and putting everyone in danger. Please let Lieutenant Nicholls know the plan for next week."

"I will. Thank you, sir," Jory said.

General Frey dismissed him, and Jory went to find Tobias. He sent Evalycer a message as he walked and almost ran into Maryllia as he did so.

"Hey!" she said, giving him a shove.

"Sorry. Glad I literally ran into you, though. We need to meet and discuss next weeks' trip to Foridian. I just sent Evalycer a message about it."

"When?" Maryllia asked.

"Later today, maybe after lunch?"

"Okay, I'll be there."

As Maryllia left, Jory got a reply back from Evalycer.

"*If I'm in town I'll be there. Not making a trip just to meet*," read the message.

"Damn it," he said. He started typing into his communicator. "*Gonna make me come to you, I see.*"

A few moments later—"*You got it. See you later.*"

"That woman," he said under his breath. He had an idea, and messaged Maryllia.

At the end of the day, Tobias and Maryllia met Jory at his land-rover and he drove them across the city to Evalycer's home. The streets were packed with vehicles and people going about their business. Jory liked driving himself places, but today maybe would have preferred someone else driving. Evalycer lived outside of Aldra, in a small but busy neighborhood.

"No wonder she didn't want to come to the base," Tobias remarked as they got out of the vehicle. "That was a trek to get here."

The house was set back ten meters from the street. It surprised Jory to see the front garden full of purple and orange plants. He hadn't figured Evalycer as being much of a gardener. Jory jogged up the steps to the door and rang the buzzer. Evalycer opened the door a moment later, dressed in something other than her work clothes. Her black tank top, loose flowing pants and her long hair slightly disheveled indicated she'd been working out.

"What are you *all* doing here?" Evalycer asked, surprised.

"I didn't want to have to repeat myself so we moved the meeting to here," Jory said, smiling. With mock concern, he said, "I hope you're not upset."

The look she gave Jory conveyed her irritation, but she said, "Of course not. Come on in." She opened the door wider and Jory went in first, followed by Maryllia and Tobias. "Can I get you anything to drink? Ennek Scotch? Red Aged? Pelonsa Reserve?"

"Yes," Jory said.

"No," Tobias and Maryllia said in unison, looking at Jory.

"I guess not," Jory said, looking at Maryllia.

Evalycer indicated for them to sit on the long couch as she pulled on a pink short-sleeved robe. She sat across from them, sipping her water.

"What's this meeting about?" she asked.

"I met with General Frey this morning," Jory started. "Next week on our run to Foridian, he wants to send a foreman and engineer along so we can meet at the Elixir facility and see how things are progressing."

"So I'm going to be the transport for the delegation, eh?" she asked.

"Looks like it. Since we'll be taking the long way around Jenubri to Foridian, it's probably the best time for them to go. We'll already have Maryllia with us, which we'll need for this as well. Maybe a couple of other people, too. We'll have to stay overnight, or maybe a couple of days."

"Well, a nice little party going on. Shall I get some hors d'oeuvres and drinks for this shindig?" she said sarcastically. "You could've told me all this in a message."

"I didn't want to just tell you this is what was going to happen, I wanted to talk with you about it."

"Do I have a choice either way?"

"No."

"Then it wouldn't have mattered."

"Of course it matters, Evalycer. I didn't want to just be a dictator and say this is how it's going to be," Jory said, his temper rising.

"Even though it is," she said.

"Look," Maryllia interjected, holding her hand up to her brother. "What Jory is trying to say is that even though this is how it is, he wanted to talk with you and see if you had any reservations or any thoughts about the trip. We're a team, and this is what teams do—talk."

"Well, I've never been much of a team player," Evalycer said. "You all know that."

"Might be time to learn," Jory said under his breath.

Evalycer glared at Jory, but said nothing to him. Looking at Tobias, she said, "The only thing I would add is another escort, more to put the passengers at ease than anything."

"I'm sure we could get Tyrian Five to come with us," Tobias said, looking to Jory.

"Sure," Jory said, still brooding.

Tobias and Maryllia looked at each other and decided it was time to go.

"We'll see you later," Maryllia said, standing up and pulling Jory to standing.

"Ever the peacemaker, Lieutenant," Evalycer said, smiling. "Thanks for dropping by."

"No problem," Tobias said. Jory didn't say anything as they left her home.

Back in the land-rover, Jory said, "That woman really gets on my nerves."

"You let her push your buttons, Jory," Maryllia told him. "You need to learn to not take her bait."

Jory sighed. "I know. It's just frustrating because she's good at what she does."

The rest of the drive back to the base was silent as Jory thought about Evalycer. As much as they had talked about the trip, he *could* have just messaged her about it. He had wanted to give her and the others the chance to ask any questions or voice any concerns.

Jory didn't get out of his vehicle once back at the base. He dropped off Maryllia and Tobias with a "We'll talk about this tomorrow," and drove home to Samara.

Once home, he helped Samara with dinner, talking about the visit with Evalycer.

"Sometimes she just drives me crazy," Jory said, stirring the sauce on the stove.

"Well, you did show up unexpectedly with Tobias and Maryllia at her home," Samara replied. "Of course she'd be taken aback."

Jory frowned. "I guess you're right. I need to remember that she is someone who wants to do things her way, regardless of anything else."

Samara came and took the sauce from Jory and poured it on the meat she had just finished cooking. "That's probably a good way to approach her."

They sat down at the table to eat. Samara talked about her day, how her class was going and her royal duties.

"Also, your mother wants us to join them for dinner tomorrow night," Samara said.

"Great. I haven't seen her or my father in a while. It will be good to see them," he said, meaning it.

The next evening after work, Jory and Samara went to the palace for dinner. Jory opened the door and he and Samara went in.

"Mother?" he called out.

Queen Arika came out of the study. "Hello! I'm so glad you could come," she said, embracing Jory first, then Samara. "It's been ages since you've been by, Jory."

"I'm sorry about that," Jory said, sheepishly. "I've been bogged down with this Elixir trade and how to get it safely to Foridian."

"Any new developments?"

"Not really. We're taking a couple of people with us next week to check on the progress of the facility there and on Yarnell.

Should be an easy trip," he said, more wishful thinking than a true statement, but he didn't want to worry his mother.

Queen Arika led them into the dining area, where King Leander and Maryllia were already seated.

"Hello, son," the king said, standing and shaking Jory's hand. He gave Samara a quick embrace before they all sat down. "How are things at the base?"

Jory quickly told him what he'd just told his mother as the staff started to bring in the first course of the meal. It had been quite a while since Jory had had a formal five-course meal. Even when he lived at the palace, he seldom made it home for dinner. He was either working or out with friends, and being married, he and Samara usually made dinner together. It was nice to be served.

As Jory and Samara prepared to leave, Queen Arika gave them a kiss on the cheek. "Come back for dinner anytime," she told them.

"We just may do that," Jory said. "Dinner was great."

King Leander shook Jory's hand, and gave Samara a hug before they got into the land-rover to drive home.

Chapter Thirteen

As the day approached for them to make their trip to Foridian, Jory and Tobias checked and rechecked the route they'd take around Jenubri. Unless the Gantians knew they were taking a different route, there shouldn't be any trouble, which Jory wanted to avoid at any cost.

Evalycer came over to the map viewer. "Making sure we'll all be safe?" she asked.

"As a matter of fact, yes," Jory said. "I don't want anything to happen while we've got passengers with us."

"It should be fine," Evalycer replied brightly. "I'm not going to broadcast our temporary route. I don't want to be responsible for anyone getting hurt."

"Good," Jory said, a little surprised at her change in attitude after the argument they'd had previously about this trip. He consulted the map viewer again. "This is the route we're taking. As you know it will take us an additional three hours around the planet. Since the foreman and engineer have to meet with the facility director and Governor while we're there, we'll be staying a day or two. That won't be a problem, will it?"

"Nope," she said. "I already figured we'd be staying since we have the construction people with us."

"Are you okay?" Jory asked.

"Yes. Why?"

"You seem a little too agreeable today."

"Well, you were right. I need to learn to be a team player."

Jory nearly choked as he started to reply. He coughed, and said, "I'm *right*?"

"Yes," Evalycer said curtly. "Don't let it go to your head."

They went over what they would need for the extra days there, then met with General Frey for scheduling. The *Silver Reign* would be loaded as usual at the base, the foreman and engineer would join the crew. Once in space, instead of going straight to the asteroid belt, they'd go slightly right. Jenubri was about the same distance from Darantha as Startia, but nearly directly in line with Darantha, which was why it added three hours to the trip. Once past Jenubri, they'd turn left and be well beyond the scanners of Startia. With any luck, they would also avoid the Gantian sensors. They would charge the weapons, just in case, and Maryllia would use her abilities to sense anything going on.

"Sounds good," Evalycer said. "I'll see you all back here in a couple of days." With a nod to the general, she left the room.

***

Evalycer didn't welcome the thought of having to stay on Foridian overnight, let alone a couple of days. But, she'd be a team player even if it killed her. Which she hoped it didn't come to that. She made sure she had everything she'd need for the trip. She traveled light, and threw a pair of work pants into her bag along with a couple of shirts and another jacket. Although she claimed to be tough, she still liked to look her best, and grabbed her make-up. Jory would probably laugh at her if he knew she had those things. Oh, well. If he laughed, he'd get punched, prince or no prince.

She looked around for her custom knife and found it on the table next to her bed. She'd wear that, just in case. Once she had everything she thought she might need, she left her home to make the drive to the base.

Once at the base, she grabbed her bag from her vehicle and went to the *Silver Reign*. She tossed her bag into the smaller hold area, then went to find Jory. Both he and Tobias were checking over their ship, as usual.

"Hey," Evalycer said.

"Good morning," Jory said. "Ready for the trip?"

"As always," she replied cheerfully. "I love being a chauffeur for people."

"And you do it so well," Jory said with a smirk.

His communicator beeped. He pulled it out and looked at the message. "The foreman and engineer are waiting for us," he said, slipping the com back into its holder. "I'm going to go meet with them, then we'll all meet at the ship in about fifteen minutes?"

"Sounds good," Evalycer said, and she went to make a few checks of her ship.

Tobias stayed with their ship while Jory went to General Frey's office.

"We heard you've been having some trouble with the locals around Ganta Zay," the foreman said, concern in his voice.

"We have," said Jory. "But we're going a different route today and we'll have an extra escort with us, so there won't be any problems. We're going around Jenubri, which adds three hours to our trip, but it's safe."

The foreman looked a little less worried. Jory knew that he'd probably never been in any kind of ship other than public transport. He hoped that Evalycer would make him and the engineer feel comfortable on the *Silver Reign*. He knew Maryllia would be diplomatic and put them at ease.

"We'll see you back in a couple of days," General Frey said.

Jory led the men to the ship and introduced them to Evalycer. She shook their hands, and took them into the ship and showed them where they could stow their bags. Maryllia came onboard a few minutes later.

"Everything set to go?" she asked, tossing her bag into the hold with the other bags.

"All set," Jory said.

Evalycer and Maryllia got the men situated while Jory went to his ship. Tobias had finished looking things over, a habit for him every time they used the ship.

"Base, this is Tyrian One," Jory said into the headset. "We're ready to go."

"Tyrian One," came the reply. "You're good to go. Stay safe."

"Will do."

Jory heard Tyrian Five and Evalycer in the headset, requesting clearance to leave as well. Both ships were cleared. Jory waited until the *Silver Reign* had cleared the hangar before he and Tyrian Five followed.

Once they got through the asteroid belt, Maryllia charged up the weapons, much to the dismay of the passengers.

"It's just a precaution," Maryllia assured them. "I'd rather be ready and nothing happen, than not be ready. We're going the long way around, and so far, it looks like we're safe. I'm going to go meditate to see into the future. I'll be in that compartment there," she said, pointing to a door across from their seats. "Knock on the door if anything happens, though I'll probably see it first."

"Thank you, your Highness," they said, forgetting her rank.

Maryllia told Evalycer and Jory of her plan. They told her they'd be on the look-out for any potential hazards as well while they flew.

Once out of the asteroid belt they started scanning the area. Jory picked up no signs of trouble from Ganta Zay from his abilities, Tobias saw nothing on the scanners. A few minutes later, Maryllia's voice came through the headset.

"I've seen nothing to worry about, Jory," she said. "All is quiet."

"Good," Jory said, relieved. "We'll soon be well beyond their scanners."

Two standard hours later, they arrived on Foridian. Governor Oxmoor met the ship with his advisor Malin Garrick and the head foreman of the construction company working on the Elixir facility.

"We'll leave you all to your visit," Jory said, shaking Governor Oxmoor's hand. "I'll be by tomorrow with the foreman to see how things are progressing."

"Good," said Oxmoor. "I look forward to it. You're all invited to my residence for dinner tonight with my wife and me."

"We'll be there," Jory said, stifling Evalycer's objections. Governor Oxmoor led the men out of the hangar to his offices.

"I don't want to go to dinner with the governor," Evalycer said crossly.

"Why not?" Jory asked.

"Not my thing."

Jory smirked. "I think you'll be surprised how these things turn out."

She sighed heavily. "Fine," she relented.

Later that evening, they all gathered at the governor's residence. A staff member led them into a formal dining hall with a huge table. Governor Oxmoor was already there with his wife, talking with the foreman and engineer.

"So glad you could all come." He gestured for them to sit around the table.

As the night went on, Evalycer became more relaxed with everyone, though still not opening up much. The governor was quite funny, and Jory and the engineer had many stories to tell.

The governor wrapped up the evening with plans for Jory to join the tour at the Elixir facility the next day.

"Good night, Governor," Jory said, shaking his hand. "We had a great time."

"My pleasure," he said, and with a wave, he shut the door.

Evalycer looked at her watch. "Night's still young," she said. "Anyone want drinks?"

"I'm not much of a night-life person," Maryllia started. "I think I'll pass for tonight."

"Good night, Maryllia," Jory said, and he watched his sister head toward their hotel.

"You guys game?" Evalycer asked.

Jory looked at Tobias, who shrugged and nodded. "Sure," Jory said.

They walked a short distance to a cantina. With its many twinkling lights, it beckoned the friends inside.

After pushing their way through the crowd, they found an empty table toward the back of the cantina. A young woman with long black hair with blue streaks and big eyes came up to them. "What can I get you?" she asked in a heavy Vistese accent.

"Pelonsa Reserve?" Evalycer asked hesitantly.

The woman wrote down her order.

Jory laughed. "Well, I'm staying away from that," he said. "I'll have an Ennek scotch."

"Same," said Tobias.

The server brought their drinks a few minutes later. Evalycer took a long drink of hers, while Jory and Tobias sipped at their drinks.

"No Reserve, huh?" Evalycer asked.

"No," Jory said, smiling sadly. "Too many bad memories associated with it."

"Yeah, I've heard about the mission you did last year. Gutsy." She held her drink up in a salute, then drank. "Princess Samara has my utmost respect for putting up with that."

"It's one I'd like to forget about."

Jory hoped that that would put an end to the questions about it. It did, as Evalycer now looked around the cantina.

"What are you looking for?" Tobias asked.

"Nothing, really," she shrugged. "Maybe a card game or something."

She finished her drink and ordered another. She thought she saw someone in the corner with a deck of cards. She grabbed her drink and walked over to check, Jory and Tobias watching carefully. Jory hoped there'd be no trouble that night.

Jory watched as Evalycer sat down and was welcomed to the game. It looked like a friendly game, so Jory didn't worry about it. He and Tobias ordered another drink each, taking in the atmosphere of the cantina.

An hour later, a commotion in the corner where Evalycer played her game made Jory and Tobias stop talking suddenly.

"Great," Jory said, standing up to investigate. He could hear Evalycer's voice above the others.

"I may be a fighter," she said. "But I'm not a cheater."

Jory and Tobias walked over to the table. Evalycer was still sitting, but another man stood with his hands on the table, leaning over to Evalycer.

"I want to see your hand," he growled. "And whatever is in your jacket."

Evalycer showed him her cards. Knowing the game she was playing, Jory could see nothing wrong with her hand.

"Take off your jacket," the man said.

"You first," Evalycer told him, unsmiling.

"I'm not taking off my jacket to show you anything," he said, his face growing red.

"Well, then," Evalycer started. "I think you're the one who's been cheating."

Evalycer stood up and shrugged off her jacket, showing nothing but her impressive blade on her belt.

"Now," she said, putting the jacket back on. "I showed you mine, so now show me yours," she said playfully, but her eyes conveyed she was not in a playful mood.

"I'm not doing it. I don't have to prove anything."

"If you have nothing to hide as I did, you would do it."

"Should we intervene?" Tobias whispered to Jory.

"No," Jory said. "She can handle herself just fine. We'll step in if needed."

The man started to back away. Evalycer drew her blade, and one of the other men at the table drew his knife. The accused man looked at Evalycer's blade nervously, and took off his jacket, a die falling to the table. Though he accused Evalycer of cheating, he'd had one of the dice in his sleeve. He would change them out when his turn came up so he would get a bad roll and lose, then

Evalycer would get a great roll. He didn't seem too bright and had planned to take her money once he had accused her of cheating. The problem was Evalycer wouldn't have given up the money without a fight. He didn't know her, didn't know her reputation, and dismissed her as just another off-lander.

"Now," Evalycer said, putting her blade back on her belt and walking around the table to get as close to him as possible. "If I were you, I'd leave before anyone else here decides you've cheated them, too. I'm sure you've done this before," she said menacingly.

"Yes, ma'am," he said, and he hurriedly stumbled around a chair, almost falling, and left the cantina.

Jory and Tobias joined in the applause and whistles from the rest of the cantina.

Evalycer took a bow, then shook hands with the other card players at the table. "Thanks for your help," she said to the man who had backed her up with his knife. She gathered up her winnings, made them into a neat bundle, and shoved them into her jacket pocket.

"Well, I think I've had enough excitement for one night," Jory said, grinning.

"Yeah, let's get out of here," Evalycer agreed.

They made their way out of the cantina and walked up the street to their hotel.

Once back on their floor, they separated to their own rooms. "Thanks for the excitement," Jory said, laughing.

"Anytime," Evalycer replied, and with a wave goodnight, she closed her door.

Jory met with the foreman and engineer after breakfast, then together with Maryllia, they went to the Elixir facility a couple kilometers outside the city. Maryllia wasn't supposed to be joining them, but Jory thought that any help with reading minds would be beneficial. He didn't expect any deception, but he was always cautious when it came to business dealings of any kind.

The construction was finished on the outside of the facility. It looked complete, but Jory knew they still had work to do on the inside. As they walked up to the door, the foreman came out to meet them.

"Glad you all are here," he said. He gave them all hard hats to wear inside the facility as he gave them the tour, telling them what they had done and still had to do. Jory glanced over at Maryllia and could see she was reading the foreman's mind as she listened to him speak.

The meeting and tour lasted half an hour. Jory thanked the foreman for his time, and the group drove back to the hotel. They contacted General Frey to report to him how the tour had gone. Both Maryllia and Jory told him that there was no deception of any kind.

"I didn't think there would be, but I wanted to be cautious," the general said. "Are you heading back today?"

"Most likely," Jory said. "No need to stay here."

"Good. We'll see you when you get back," General Frey said, and his face faded from view.

Jory went to tell Evalycer the good news that they would leave that day for home.

"Great," she said. "I've been bored to death while waiting for your meeting to be over."

"The meeting went quicker than I expected," Jory admitted. "I thought we'd be here all day."

Jory met with the governor one last time before they went to the ship for the trip home. "Thank you for your hospitality," Jory said, shaking Governor Oxmoor's hand.

"We'll see you next week," said the governor.

Chapter Fourteen

General Frey called Jory and Evalycer into his office.

"We've got another problem," Frey said.

"What now?" Evalycer asked.

"You can't go around Jenubri this week to avoid Ganta Zay and Startia."

"Why not?" Jory asked.

"They are entering their magnetic storm period," the general said. "No one can fly near there for eight days. That leaves flying past Startia or dealing with the pirates and Keedu."

"What does the universe have against us?" Evalycer asked. "Not great options here."

"Neither way is ideal," Jory said. "But we know what to expect with the Gantians. We have no idea what that faction will do to any of us if we fly past Startia and they intercept us. I say we take the direct route."

Jory looked at Evalycer, who looked relieved.

"Thanks," Evalycer said.

"I'll contact Governor Oxford and have his pilots ready to go when we make the trip," General Frey said.

As they left the general's office, Jory said, "They've really got you scared."

"That faction on Startia?" she asked. "Yeah, they do. Not just for me, but they've threatened my parents, too." She looked around to make sure no one could hear them. "They are the *one* thing that scares me enough to quit this job. I'll take on Keedu any day over the faction."

***

Evalycer got ready for the weekly trip to Foridian, checking out the ship, making sure everything was in top shape. She'd had a vision of something going wrong and wanted to know her ship was ready. When Jory came in later that morning, he wanted to speak with both Evalycer and Maryllia right away.

"I saw something this morning during my meditation," Jory started.

"I did, too," Maryllia said.

"So did I," Evalycer replied.

Jory looked at her sharply. "You did?"

"I actually have more going for me than strength and sheer gutsiness," she told him.

"We need to be prepared for anything. I'm not even going to try to talk you out of going, Maryllia," he said, looking at his sister.

"Good," she said laconically.

"Xander isn't going with us today," Evalycer told them. "He broke his ankle yesterday and can't fly for two days."

"Great," Jory said sarcastically. "Do you have someone to replace him?"

"I couldn't find anyone willing to go. I'll have Aiden take a laser canon if needed."

At the usual part of the trip, outside of the asteroid belt, Maryllia and Evalycer charged up the weapons. Everyone was on a heightened sense of alert. Aiden looked as if he'd puke any minute.

"Incoming!" Evalycer exclaimed.

Jory looked out his window and saw the fighters from Ganta Zay coming in. "How did we not pick them up on our scanners?" he asked.

"I don't know, but they're coming fast," Evalycer replied, nudging her controller forward to try to get more speed out of the huge ship. Aiden flipped some switches to try to divert more power to the engines. The engines responded slightly, but they were not going to outrun those fighters.

Maryllia ran down to her weapon station and strapped herself into the chair. She turned on the screen and watched as the fighters got closer.

"Don't fire on them unless they do so first," Jory said into the headset.

"Copy that," Maryllia said.

"I'm going to try to intercept them and maybe head them off," Jory said, turning his fighter into the oncoming battle. "We need to contact Foridian and get their fighters out here to help."

Tobias pushed a button on his console to contact Foridian. "Copy that," he said into the headset, then turned to Jory. "They'll be here in five minutes."

Laser fire rocked their fighter. Jory and Tobias rolled their fighter out of the way of more laser fire. Maryllia fired the laser cannons at them, and Evalycer and Aiden did what they could with their guns.

The Gantian fighters started to surround the *Silver Reign*, firing over the cockpit, trying to make them turn toward Ganta Zay. Evalycer held her course.

"Foridian, this is Tyrian One," Jory said. "Are your fighters close? We're under attack."

"Tyrian One, this is Foridian base," Came the reply. "Fighters should be there any minute now."

Jory and Tobias guided their fighter nearer the *Silver Reign*, trying to keep the Gantians at bay. The Foridian fighters came blazing in, weapons firing on the Gantians.

Evalycer tried to keep the *Silver Reign* on course, but it was becoming difficult. The Gantian fighters persisted. They flew at the ship or fired at them, just missing, making them turn toward Ganta Zay. Evalycer would correct her course, and other fighters came in.

"We're having a hell of a time staying on course," Evalycer said into the headset.

"They've got all of us engaged," Jory said, again trying to go after the fighters. "Every time I try to break off, they come after us."

"I thought you were the best the RPF had," Evalycer said impertinently.

"I can't hold them *all* off," he said.

Another signal appeared on their screens.

"What *is* that?" Tobias asked, stunned.

None of them had seen the ship coming toward them. The ship was twice as big as the *Silver Reign*. Jory and the other fighters started firing at it, but had no impact on it.

"It must have a cloaking device," Jory said. "We would have seen that behemoth coming at us."

"I'm sure it's made out of that duratatium as well," Evalycer said. "Our laser fire isn't doing a damn thing."

The Gantian fighters started firing again at the *Silver Reign*, moving it toward the ship.

Jory realized too late that they had all gotten too close to the monstrosity as he felt the pull of the tractor beam. The fighters had driven them all into tractor beam range. The *Silver Reign* fought the pull of the beam.

"Evalycer, you're just going to burn up your engines," Jory said.

"Yes, listen to your leader," came a deep voice in their headsets.

"Who is this?" Jory demanded.

"I am Keedu. I am the ruler of Ganta Zay."

"Well, Keedu, you will let us go now, or all your pilots out here will be destroyed," Jory told him.

"Like this?" Keedu said, and the Gantian fighters each launched a laser at most of the Foridian fighters.

Jory's eyes widened in surprise as he gasped at the destruction of the Foridian fighters. He had never seen anything like that. He'd seen ships destroyed, but none with the ease as those ships seemed to have been destroyed. They were nearly disintegrated.

"Do I have your attention?" Keedu asked.

110

"Yes," Jory said.

"What the hell, Jory?" Evalycer asked "You're not going to listen to him, are you?"

"Did you see what he just did to those fighters? Be quiet," he snapped.

"Before you try to use your weapons, we have rendered them inoperable. All we want is the Elixir ship," Keedu said. "We have no use for your ship, Major Vance."

"How do you know my name?"

"We've done our research. Now, in a moment, you will be released from the tractor beam, and we will use our repulsor beam to move you toward the asteroid belt. If you attempt to come back toward this ship or Ganta Zay, you will be destroyed just like those fighters."

Jory sat quietly, trying to think. He didn't see any way out of this, nor any way to help the *Silver Reign*.

"You can try and think of a way to help," said Keedu, sensing Jory's hesitance. "But we will destroy you if you try anything."

"Shit."

"I take it by your profanity that you understand."

Jory sighed, defeated. "Yes."

"We can't just leave them," Tobias said, urgency in his voice.

"If you have a better idea, I'm listening," Jory said.

"Jory," Maryllia said. "Just go. We'll figure something out." She sounded determined, but the shaking in her voice made Jory uneasy.

Jory felt their fighter being released from the tractor beam, then taken over by the repulsor beam, forcing them toward the asteroid belt. The repulsor beam's reach stopped a hundred kilometers short of the belt. Jory had thoughts of turning around and going back, but he knew there'd be no way they'd survive.

He'd seen what those lasers did to the Foridian fighters. He kept on his present course toward home.

"Foridian base, this is Tyrian One," Jory said into his headset.

"This is Foridian base," came the reply.

"We're headed home. I don't know if you saw or heard anything that just happened…"

"We saw the battle and that ship and what they did to our fighters," said Governor Oxmoor, his voice strained. "Don't try to come back and help us. Take care of yourselves and figure out your next plan of action. We'll do what we can, but against something that powerful…" his voice faded off.

***

The Gantian ship pulled the *Silver Reign* into the hanger bay on Ganta Zay, into what looked like their main city. Maryllia watched over the shoulders of Evalycer and Aiden, and had a thought. She ran back to the small cargo hold and brought out three cans of Elixir and took them up to the cockpit. "Here," she said, shoving the cans into their hands. "Drink these quickly. If we're here any length of time, our abilities will start to diminish. This will help us keep them for another day."

They drank them down quickly, finishing just as the *Silver Reign* was deposited on the floor of the cavernous hanger bay. The bigger ship also landed a few meters away. The hangar bay doors closed with a loud scraping of metal.

Several rugged, ragged looking men surrounded the ship's exit door, pointing their guns at the door.

"Well, this doesn't look good," Evalycer observed. She tried to think of something to get them out of this mess, but there really was no way. They'd be blown to bits before they could even get out of tractor beam range if they could even get out of the hangar bay. The three of them couldn't take on all fifteen men out there.

"We're screwed," Aiden said. "We're totally screwed."

"Don't panic," Evalycer whispered. "Just keep your cool and watch our lead." She looked at Maryllia. "You ready?"

"As ready as I'll ever be," she said, trying to smile.

"Pilot," one of the men shouted. "Open the exit door and come out slowly, hands up."

"See ya," Evalycer said. She went back and opened the door, and raised her hands as she walked down the ramp. The men grabbed her by the arms and forced her to her knees. The man shouted for Aiden and Maryllia to do the same. They did so, Aiden throwing up on the way out. Evalycer rolled her eyes. One of the men shoved Maryllia to her knees as another man pulled her arms back behind her and held them there. They did the same to Aiden, wiping off his face as they did so. The Gantians took their captives' weapons off their belts, Evalycer keeping a sharp eye on her blade.

A tall, dark-haired man wearing a vest over his dirty blue shirt, several belts of weapons, and holding a laser rifle stepped out from the group of men. He, as well as the others, had a mask dangling around his neck. He walked over to Evalycer and looked down at her with his piercing cold gray eyes.

"You are the pilot?" he asked gruffly.

"Yes," Evalycer snapped.

"I expected someone…"

"A man, perhaps?" she interrupted.

"Possibly. But more of someone who was older. Bigger," he sneered. The men behind him laughed.

"I may be small, but you don't want to tangle with me."

"Is that so? Well, we'll see about that later on," Keedu said, looking her over suggestively. He moved over to Aiden. "Who are you?"

"The c-co-pilot," Aiden managed to say without barfing again. He was shaking, and sweating profusely. Barely old enough to be a pilot, Aiden had never been in any kind of danger as a pilot until now.

"You're not going to vomit again, are you?"

"N-no," Aiden said, though he looked like he would at any moment.

"And who are you?" the man said, moving to Maryllia.

"Security," she told him.

"You have the uniform of the Royal Planet Fighters. What is your rank?"

"What's it to you?"

"Just curious. I want to know if they sent their best or a lackey to keep the ship secure."

"Lieutenant."

"Well, Lieutenant, I don't think you were very much help on this trip, were you?" Again, the men laughed.

"You'd be surprised."

The man stepped back to address all three of them. "I am Keedu. I run this place."

"What do you want with us?" Evalycer asked.

"We want your shipment of the Elixir," Keedu said. He started pacing as he spoke. "As you can see, we are just a poor people here. We trade our duratatium with other planets in exchange for food, but we need more to survive. As you've probably noticed, the air here isn't very breathable. We cannot make our air clean because of the mining process for the duratatium. We want to negotiate for the Elixir."

"What use is the Elixir to you?" Maryllia asked.

"I think the Elixir will benefit us as we try to acquire certain, uh, shipments."

"You mean take what's not yours," Evalycer said.

"We manage as best as we can, and if we have to take things to help us survive, then so be it."

"Well, that ain't gonna happen," Evalycer stated matter-of-factly.

"Oh, it will, if Darantha wants its princess back."

Evalycer looked sharply at Maryllia, who looked stunned.

"Yes, we know who you are, your highness," Keedu said, smiling salaciously. Maryllia shifted nervously on her knees. "And if you want to go back home with your friends, you'll convince your government to keep sending us Elixir shipments each week."

"This isn't the way to go about getting the Elixir," Maryllia said. "What makes you think they'll negotiate with you after the way we've been treated?"

"We haven't hurt you yet," Keedu said.

"You've captured us and taken us hostage," said Evalycer. "Not the best way to open a conversation about this."

"I'll deal with Darantha later," Keedu said, turning to his men. "Take them to the habitation block. Give them the nicest habitat and everything they need."

Keedu's men lifted Evalycer, Maryllia, and Aiden roughly to stand, and with laser rifles at their backs, they followed two other men down the corridor to an elevator. They all stepped in, and one man pushed a button. The elevator jerked upward.

The elevator stopped a few moments later and the doors opened. The men nudged the group out the doors and into the glass-covered hallway. They followed the men down the hallway, looking out at the city as they walked. A thick brown haze covered the area and the people below all wore masks over their faces to protect them from the polluted air. Their sun barely penetrated the haze, giving the air an orange-brown glow.

They stopped the hostages at a door. One of the men input a code and the door opened. The habitat was minimally furnished, but comfortable enough for the three of them. A couch sat along one wall with a table in front of it, with a chair and a side table. A kitchen off one side of the living area and a bedroom with four beds and a bathroom off the other side rounded out the habitat. The place was dim, as very little light came through the windows, but it seemed clean.

"You'll stay here until Keedu wants you," said one of the men. He took the restraints off their wrists and backed out of the room and locked the door after them.

Chapter Fifteen

Jory contacted General Frey once his fighter passed the asteroid belt.

"This is Base," came the reply.

"General, the Gantians have seized the *Silver Reign*," he said. "We were all caught in the tractor beam. We had help from Foridian, but the fire power was too much for our ships." He stopped to steady his voice. "Sir, they blew up several of the Foridian fighters and told us that if we didn't leave, they'd do the same to us. They have a repulsor beam that sent us as near to the asteroid belt as they could get us, and told us not to return."

"We'll get started on a plan here," said the general. "Once you're back, we'll debrief you and figure out a strategy to get them back."

"Copy that," Jory said.

***

Evalycer looked around. "Cozy," she said sarcastically.

"How did they know who I was?" Maryllia asked.

"They probably already knew who we were before they brought us in," Evalycer said, looking out the window. She had a sudden thought. "Those scans. They scanned us when they scanned the shipment and found out who we were."

"What are we going to do?" Aiden whined.

Evalycer turned to snap at him, but his colorless skin and wide-eyed look made her soften her stance.

"We'll get out of this, don't worry," Evalycer said. "What abilities do you have, Aiden?"

"Um, I have strength and speed," he said. "And sometimes mind reading if the person is close by."

"Okay, good. Maryllia, I know you have mind reading; what else?"

"Seeing into the future, telekinesis, some strength ability," Maryllia said.

"I have mind reading, strength, telekinesis, and seeing into the future. I think we have everything covered. We need to figure out some way to get out of here."

They had a plan in place by the time the men came back for them an hour later. The men led them down to the control room, where Keedu already had General Frey on the communicator screen.

"We told you before," General Frey said. "We don't negotiate with criminals."

"Not even to get your princess back?" Keedu asked.

"I want to see them," Frey demanded.

One of the men pushed the three of them into view.

"As you can see, they are unharmed," Keedu said. "But that can change at any moment if I don't get what I want."

General Frey frowned. "Give us an hour to discuss this."

"One hour," Keedu said, and he pushed the button, ending the communication. He turned to Evalycer, Aiden, and Maryllia. "I guess you have one hour to see who lives and who dies."

Maryllia glared at Keedu, as Aiden turned a pale shade of green. Evalycer cleared her throat. "I need to speak with you, Keedu," she said.

"Why do you want to speak to *him*?" Maryllia asked.

"I may be able to help him," she said.

"How can you help me?" Keedu barked.

"I can get the Elixir to you," Evalycer said.

"What are you doing?" Maryllia said. "This wasn't part of the plan, Evalycer."

"Sayzan," Keedu said, turning to the man standing next to him with the long, brown hair. "Take these two back to their room. I want to talk to this one."

Sayzan nudged Maryllia and Aiden out the door, the door sliding shut behind them.

"Now," Keedu said. "What do you think you can do for me? I know there's a few things I can think of that you can do for me," he said. The other men laughed and whistled.

"Ha ha," Evalycer said sarcastically. "That ain't gonna happen. But I can get the Elixir to you—for the right price."

"Aren't you a member of the RPF?"

"Do I look like a member of the RPF?" she asked incredulously. "No, I hire out to the highest bidder. That's why I'm working *for* the RPF, not *with* them. They pay their contractors very well."

Keedu stood up and paced the floor, thinking. Evalycer could see him mulling it over in his head. "How would you get the Elixir? I'm sure you can't just get a shipment of it to take anytime you want."

"I have my ways of getting things, much like you," she said.

"I'll think about it. Take her back to the room."

Sayzan had returned and took Evalycer back to the room.

"How'd it go?" Maryllia asked after Sayzan shut and locked the door again.

"He said he'd think about it," Evalycer shrugged. "I was pretty convincing, but I think he doubts that I can get the Elixir for him." She headed to the bathroom. "I need a shower after the way he looked me over. Made me want to gouge his eyes out."

***

Keedu thought about the pilot's proposal. It would be easier to get it from her instead of hijacking the shipments. Who was this woman? Did she have the connections she said she had? He sat down at his desk and punched in her name into his computer. Of course her record with the RPF came up. Lieutenant, decorated interrogator, pilot. He didn't see anything there that would lead him to believe she could get the Elixir for him.

Keedu contacted his man on Foridian, to tell him about this new development.

"She says she can get the Elixir for us, for a price," Keedu said into the communicator. "But nothing I've seen would indicate she can do this."

"Let me do some digging," the man said. "I may be able to get further than you can, since I'm not using an enemy's computer."

Keedu waited only a few minutes before his man contacted him again.

"She's got quite a history," the man said. "While she was the one who protected the governor on Startia, she's also wanted there by a faction who had plotted to kill Atouu."

"That is interesting," Keedu said thoughtfully.

"If they were to find her, they would capture her and possibly kill her."

"So that's why they take the long way to Foridian, to avoid us and Startia. I think we can use this information to our advantage."

* * *

Once Jory and Tobias were back on Darantha, the general briefed them on the communication from Keedu.

"Do they honestly think we'd make a deal with them?" Tobias asked incredulously. "They're pirates and criminals."

"We have to make them think we're going to negotiate with them," the general said. "I know your parents will want to do anything to get your sister back, Major Vance, but we need to not give in to what they want."

"I need to go tell them what's happened," Jory said.

"Yes," said Frey. "Let them know we will formulate a plan to get her and the others back safely."

Tobias offered to go with Jory to inform the king and queen about the capture. Jory welcomed the company. The ride to the palace was silent, though, as Jory thought about how his parents would react. He knew his father would want to give them anything to get Maryllia back. He hoped his mother would have a calmer head and think the situation through.

They arrived at the palace and Jory and Tobias went inside. They found Queen Arika in her office working on her computer.

"Hello, Mother," Jory greeted.

"Jory!" the queen said. She stood up and embraced her son. "Hello, Tobias," the queen said.

"Your majesty," Tobias said, with a nod of his head. He took the queen's outstretched hand to shake.

"What brings you both here in the middle of the day?" she asked.

"Is Father here?" Jory asked.

"That never means anything good," Queen Arika said, turning serious. She led them to King Leander's office across the hallway. She knocked on the door and the king beckoned them in.

"Jory's got something to talk to us about," the queen told him.

"What's going on?' the king asked.

"While we were on our way to Foridian today," Jory started. "We were intercepted by Gantian fighters. They had laser fire that was more powerful than we've ever seen. They drove us into their tractor beam range. The *Silver Reign* and our fighter got pulled in, but they let us go."

"What about your sister?" the queen asked.

"They took her, the pilot and co-pilot hostage on Ganta Zay. The Gantians want the Elixir as trade for their duratatium on their planet, then they will release the hostages."

King Leander stood up and came around his desk. "Then we give them what they want."

"We can't do that, Father," Jory said firmly. "If we do that, then those pirates will be more powerful. They don't want to trade for the duratatium. They just wanted the Elixir."

"Lee," said Queen Arika. "We have to let the RPF figure out a strategy to get them back without bowing to their wishes."

"But it's our daughter!"

"Maryllia is trained for this, Lee. And it sounds like the pilot can hold her own as well. We need to let General Frey and the RPF take control of this."

"You're right, as always," King Leander said. "I'm going to go to the base to see what their strategy is."

"I'll be there in a while," Jory said. "I need to let Samara know that I'm going to be busy at the base with this."

He and Tobias went to Jory's home. They found Samara in her office working on her charity work. Tobias waited in the living room.

"You're back!" she said, rising from her chair to kiss him.

Jory kissed her quickly, and said, "We have a situation."

"Oh, no," Samara replied.

Jory quickly gave Samara the information on what had happened and what they needed to do now.

"I wanted to let you know that I won't be home for a while. If you wanted, I'm sure you could stay at the palace."

"I'm okay here," Samara said. "The staff will look after me."

"I'll try to come home tomorrow, but I may not be able to get a break. I'll sleep at the base."

"Be careful, Jory."

"I will." He kissed her goodbye. He and Tobias drove back to the base. King Leander was already there in the control room with General Frey.

"Good, you're here," General Frey said as Jory entered the room. He turned back to the group of men and women. "We've been contacted by Keedu, the leader of Ganta Zay. He confirmed what Major Vance said—they want the Elixir. They will not release the hostages until they get what they want. We're not going to give them that, but we're going to let them think they are getting what they want."

"How do you plan to do that?" Jory asked.

"They have the shipment of Elixir right now. They won't release the hostages until we make a deal with them to supply them with the Elixir. We need to somehow give them a 'good faith' Elixir shipment, but only if they release the hostages," Frey said.

"They won't release the hostages with just that, will they?" King Leander asked.

"We may get one hostage back. We can negotiate to get your daughter back..."

"They'll want to keep her because of who she is," Jory interjected.

"We can have some troops on the freighter," Captain Fletcher suggested. "We can somehow keep them hidden on board until the Elixir is unloaded, then we strike."

"That's a good idea," Jory said. "But they have those scanners that can tell them who's on the ship. We'll have to do this with minimal help."

***

Evalycer had been looking around the room to see if there was any way out. There wasn't of course, since they were several hundred meters up in the air. Even if they did escape from the room, in order to go outside, they'd need masks.

"We'll have to see what they have in store for us when they come back," Maryllia said. "Our plan will depend on that."

123

With that, they decided to find out how to get food from the food dispenser. Evalycer pushed a button and spoke into the speaker, requesting some fruit. The lights on the dispenser started to blink, and a moment later, the chute opened and fruit dropped out into the tray below.

"Hmm," Evalycer said, taking the fruit out of the tray and looking it over. "Think it's safe to eat?"

"I don't think they're going to poison us," Maryllia said. "They need us to get what they want."

Evalycer bit into a small, purple berry. It was juicy and sweet.

"Tastes okay," she said, and she tossed one to Maryllia and to Aiden, who both ate heartily.

They found water in the refrigerator and drank that down. They had nothing else to do afterwards but watch the traffic and people outside, or rest. Aiden slept on the couch, but Evalycer and Maryllia sat facing each other, silently thinking of a way to get out of there.

A few hours later, the door opened and three men stood in the doorway. "Keedu wants to speak with you now," the tallest man said.

Evalycer, Maryllia, and Aiden stood up and walked to the door. "Turn around," the man barked. They turned around and the man put restraints back on their wrists before letting them out into the hallway.

Led by Sayzan, they followed him down the hall to the elevator, going up to the top of the building. The doors opened and they were pushed out and led to an office at the end of another hallway. Sayzan hit a button, and a buzzer sounded inside the room. The door slid open, and they saw Keedu sitting at a wooden table. The room was dingy, with one overhead light giving off minimal light for the room.

"Sit down," Keedu ordered.

Maryllia, Evalycer, and Aiden sat down in the chairs directly in front of the table. The three of them waited for Keedu to speak. He continued to scribble on the electronic tablet on his table.

As she sat and waited for Keedu to speak, Maryllia glanced around at her crew. Hanging his head, Aiden looked defeated. He stared at the floor, chest heaving, chin trembling. She wanted to assure him that everything would be okay, but at that point, even she wasn't sure what would happen. To her left, Evalycer held her head high, looking directly at Keedu, stoic as ever. Maryllia hoped her own face conveyed firm determination, though she didn't feel it.

Keedu moving his tablet aside brought Maryllia out of her thoughts.

"I need you to teach me how to use the Elixir, Princess," Keedu said.

"Don't call me 'Princess'," she snapped. Maryllia hated being called Princess like it was her name.

"Oh, a little sensitive, are we?" he mocked, looking up from his work. "Okay, *Lieutenant,* I need to know how to use this and what to expect."

"You drink it," she said sarcastically.

"If you get smart with me, I *will* hurt you," he said coldly. "I'm going to drink the Elixir no matter what you tell me. You might as well tell me what will happen."

"How about we just let you drink it and see if you die?" Evalycer declared. "Maybe your genetic make-up doesn't tolerate the Elixir."

"There has never been anyone who has died from it," Keedu said. "I've done my research on that. Now, tell me what to expect, or should I start shooting," he said, and he pulled out his laser rifle and started randomly waving it around.

"Half an hour after drinking it," Maryllia started quickly. She didn't want Aiden to panic and throw up again. "You'll feel things becoming clearer. After an hour or so, you'll start feeling things happen. Depending on your genetics, you may suddenly crush something in your hand, you may be able to read minds or see things in the future. You may make things jump around on your desk or in the room. It depends," she shrugged.

"How long until I can control these powers?"

"I don't know."

Keedu got up quickly from this chair and went around the table. He grabbed Maryllia's neck and pulled her out of her chair, nearly lifting her off her feet. She started to gag and cough, but with her hands behind her she couldn't do anything but kick her feet as she struggled to get out of his grip.

"I'm tired of your games, Princess," he said through clenched teeth. "Tell me what I need to know!"

Maryllia couldn't say anything, but she focused on Keedu's stomach area, and he dropped her as he doubled over in pain. As quickly as the pain came, it was gone.

"What did you do?" Keedu asked, straightening up again, his hand still on his stomach.

"Something I learned from Count Radern of Ornocto," she told him, gasping for air. "Hurts, doesn't it?"

Keedu smiled. "I look forward to learning everything I can. Now, how long until I can control these powers?"

"It can take as long as a month to fully control your abilities," Maryllia told him. "You will need direction on how to do it."

"That's why I have you," he told her.

"We're not going to tell you a damn thing," Evalycer said.

Keedu looked at her, almost like an afterthought. "I will get what I need, no matter the price." He studied Evalycer for a moment until she started to squirm under his stare. "I've decided I'm not going to take you up on your offer, Lieutenant," he said, emphasizing the rank.

"I told you, I'm not an officer with the RPF anymore," Evalycer said.

"I think we can still use you, however. I'll get back with you later."

Keedu motioned for his men to take them back to their room. Once back at their room, the men took off the restraints and locked them back into their room.

"What was that about?" Maryllia asked.

"I have no idea," Evalycer replied. "All I told him earlier was what we planned."

Chapter Sixteen

General Frey contacted Keedu telling him that they would send a small shipment of the Elixir to Ganta Zay, but only if they released a hostage. Keedu had the hostages brought into the communication room.

"We want you to release Lieutenant Vance," Frey told him.

"I don't think we can do that," Keedu said slowly. "I need her to help us learn to control our abilities. I'll give you the co-pilot. He's no use to me. I'm keeping the princess and the pilot."

"No princess, no deal," the general said.

Keedu pulled Aiden up and held the blaster to his head. Aiden started to hyperventilate and almost fainted, but managed to not completely fall apart. "How about I *don't* return this one and just get rid of him?"

General Frey shook his head. "You'll get your shipment."

Keedu pushed Aiden back to the floor. "I'll expect it today."

"We can't get it there until tomorrow. We have to get the order together and find a pilot willing to transport it there, since you've got our best pilot there with you. We can get it there tomorrow as early as we can," he hurriedly added as Keedu started to pull Aiden into view again. "It's the best we can do."

Keedu looked at Evalycer, who nodded. "What he said is true. I was doing these runs because I'm the best, so they will have to try to find someone quickly to do the run here."

"Okay," he said. "I will see you here tomorrow, and we will release the boy."

The general's picture faded from view. Keedu turned to his hostages. "Any funny business tomorrow, and none of you will leave here in one piece." He turned to his men. "Sayzan, take them back to their quarters."

Sayzan motioned them ahead of him, and they walked the familiar route back to their rooms. Sayzan took off the binders and pushed them into the room and locked the door.

"We need to formulate a plan," Evalycer said.

"You heard what Keedu said," Aiden whined. "None of us will get to leave."

"He's planning on us losing our abilities overnight," Maryllia said. "We'll still have about twelve hours left tomorrow because we drank the Elixir before we were taken hostage."

"Brilliant thinking, by the way," Evalycer said.

"I learned a few things from my brother's mission last year."

***

General Frey got a small shipment of the Elixir ready for pick-up the next day while Jory and Tobias looked for a pilot to take the shipment to Ganta Zay. No outside pilot wanted to do it, so Jory started asking around the base. No one there was eager to do it, either, but would do it if ordered. Jory didn't want to order someone to do it, but would if needed.

Captain Fletcher came up to him. "We'll do it," he said, indicating himself and his co-pilot, Lieutenant Yates.

"You know what you're getting into, right?" Jory asked.

"Yes," Fletcher said. "I think you'll also need us—to back you up if anything goes wrong."

"Having someone experienced would be helpful," Jory agreed.

By the time Jory found Fletcher and Yates to help out, General Frey had gotten the Elixir order ready, and secured a small freighter to take it to Ganta Zay.

"We'll need to get going at first light," Jory said. "We'll be your escort. Hopefully, they let us land with you."

"I'm sure you'll persuade them to let you land," Fletcher said with a smirk.

They made plans to meet at the base at 0400 the next morning, and Jory went home to see Samara.

He arrived home a few minutes later and went in where he found Samara in the sunroom, reading. She looked up when she heard Jory enter the room and smiled.

"I thought I wouldn't see you until tomorrow," she said, setting her reading tablet on the side table. She got up and met him in the middle of the room.

"I was able to get away for the night after all," he said, kissing her. "I'm leaving early tomorrow morning to take a shipment of the Elixir to Ganta Zay."

"Who's going with you?"

"Tobias, of course, and Captain Fletcher and Lieutenant Yates. We're hoping to get at least one hostage back."

"Are you hungry? I can warm up something for you."

"I just want you," he said, kissing her passionately. He held her face in his hands, kissing her, then pushed his hands up through her hair, tempering his kisses. Jory picked her up and carried her to their bedroom, where he kicked the door shut and lay Samara on the bed. He needed to feel her, taste her, be with her before things heated up with getting the hostages back.

He felt the stress leave his body with every kiss of her lips and every touch of her hands. The scent of her hair intoxicated him, making him forget everything but that moment with her.

As they climaxed, he felt the last of the tension leave his body. They lay unmoving on the bed, catching their breath, very much relaxed. He found the energy to brush Samara's hair from her face and smiled.

"I love you," he whispered.

"I love you, too" she said, her hand resting on his cheek.

It was still dark the next morning when Jory got up, making sure to not wake Samara. He drank down a can of Elixir before grabbing a piece of fruit and some bread to eat on the way to the base. When he arrived at the base, he checked his messages before going to his ship to check it out. Tobias was already there, doing the pre-flight checks.

"Everything look good?" Jory asked.

"Yep," Tobias said. "We're good to go whenever everyone is here."

A few minutes later, Fletcher and Yates came across the hangar bay to meet with them. They went over the plan again, making sure everyone knew their part in it.

General Frey came over as they got ready to leave. "Be careful," he told them. "This Keedu sounds like he'll do anything to get the Elixir."

"Yes, sir," Jory said. "We'll be on our guard once we get there."

Jory and Tobias climbed into their fighter as Fletcher and Yates went to their ship, a small freighter called the *Noble*. When everyone was ready, the *Noble* started its way out of the hangar bay. Jory and Tobias followed in their fighter.

Once clear of Darantha, they made the jump to light speed. Time was of the essence, and Jory worried about his sister and the crew of the *Silver Reign*. He knew that both Maryllia and Evalycer were capable of holding their own, but his concern was with Aiden and with Keedu. As much as he disliked Aiden, Jory knew that he was just a kid, and not used to all the hostilities. It concerned Jory that Keedu would somehow take advantage of Aiden's fear and use it.

"We're coming up on the asteroid belt," Tobias said, interrupting Jory's thoughts

"Bring us into sub-light speed," he said. Tobias did, and they took control of the ship. They saw the *Noble* also cut into sub-light speed.

"Almost there," Jory told Fletcher.

Jory contacted the security outpost to get the escort through the asteroids. Once through, instead of their usual route to Foridian and trying to avoid Ganta Zay, they headed toward the planet.

"Doesn't look very inviting," Fletcher said, noticing the brown haze around the planet as they got closer.

They got within a few hundred kilometers and felt the pull of the tractor beam.

"Do you have the Elixir?" Keedu asked.

"Yes, we do," Jory said.

"We will pull you into our hangar bay, where we will inspect the shipment to make sure there is nothing wrong with it."

"Copy that."

None of them had to do anything as the tractor beam brought the ships into the hangar bay. They were instructed to come out of their ships with their hands on top of their heads. Jory and Tobias did so, as did Fletcher and Yates from the *Noble*. Jory couldn't believe that none of them were put into restraints.

"I realize that any one of you can hurt any one of us, just by using your abilities," Keedu said as he came forward. "Your sister has already demonstrated that, Major Vance," he said, stopping in front of Jory.

"Atta girl," he said, grinning broadly.

"She is very good with her abilities," Keedu continued. "But they should be wearing off fairly soon, since they haven't drunk the Elixir today, and will not be doing so."

"Where are they?" Jory asked, turning serious. "I want to see them all."

Keedu motioned for Sayzan to get the crew from their rooms. As they waited, Keedu told Jory and his men to lower their arms. "I've got several blasters pointed in your direction," Keedu said. "Don't try anything."

A few minutes later, the guards brought Maryllia, Evalycer, and Aiden out to the hangar bar. None of them looked the worse for wear, though Aiden seemed anxious.

"Jory!" Maryllia exclaimed when she saw her brother.

"Are you all okay?" he asked.

"We're fine," Evalycer said. "Aiden's been a little sick, but dealing with these creeps will do that to a person."

Keedu nodded, and Sayzan jabbed Evalycer in the stomach with the end of his laser rifle. She doubled over in pain, and so did Sayzan. Jory saw Maryllia stare at Sayzan, then she looked away and Sayzan stopped grimacing.

"How are you still able to do that?" Keedu demanded. "Your abilities should have worn off by now."

"I'm a resourceful person," Maryllia shrugged.

Jory tried to delve into her mind, and found that they had drunk a can of Elixir right before they were captured. He nodded his approval to her.

"Seems like you don't know everything about the Elixir, do you," Jory said.

Keedu's face grew red with anger. "If you want any of my hostages released, you all had better play nice."

Evalycer stood upright again. Jory gave her a look that said she needed to listen to Keedu.

"We'll behave," Evalycer said.

"Good. Now, it looks like the Elixir shipment is in order. I will give you one hostage. Who should it be?" Keedu asked rhetorically, strolling in front of each of the hostages.

"Aiden," Maryllia and Evalycer said in unison.

"Yes," Keedu replied thoughtfully, stroking his chin. "He hasn't been well since we captured him. I think this has been a bit much for him. Aiden, you're free to leave."

Aiden looked at Jory, then at Keedu, who nodded. Aiden started slowly across the space between him and Jory's group, then walked faster once he realized that no one was going to stop him.

Jory patted him on the shoulder, and whispered, "Get onto the ship." Aiden nearly ran to the *Noble* and went up the ramp.

"Now, how about we talk about releasing these two?" Jory asked.

"There will be no negotiation," Keedu said. "I need the princess to help me learn about the Elixir, and I'm keeping the other one because she's feisty and entertaining."

"Oh, brother," Evalycer said, rolling her eyes.

"We're not leaving without them," Jory said firmly.

"Then you won't be leaving any time soon, will you?" Keedu told him. Keedu's men raised their weapons higher.

"Jory, just go," Maryllia said. "We'll be out of here before you know it."

"That is true," he said. At those words, Fletcher and Yates started firing their blasters, Jory tossed a blaster to Maryllia, who started shooting and running. Evalycer, using her Strength ability, ran at Keedu, pushed him down, and grabbed her knife off his weapons belt, Tobias tossing a blaster to her as she ran.

"Jory!" came a shout in the chaos. He looked over and saw that Sayzan had grabbed Maryllia around the waist and was dragging her back toward the group of men. Momentarily distracted, he felt laser fire burn through him, though only grazing the top of his shoulder. He aimed in the direction of the laser blast and stopped. Sayzan and Keedu had pulled Maryllia in front of themselves as a shield, the blaster on the floor in front of them. Jory raised his hands, signaling a cease-fire.

Keedu grabbed his knife from his belt, and held it up to Maryllia's throat. "Leave now," he said tersely. "Or I kill her."

"Fuck," he said under his breath.

Evalycer stood behind him, breathing heavily, her blaster aimed in Keedu's direction.

"I can take him, Jory," she said.

Keedu and his men outgunned them, even with Evalycer's weapon. Twenty of Keedu's men had their weapons trained on the five of them.

Jory slowly lowered his weapon and pushed Evalycer's down. The other men in the rescue group did the same.

"You're not going to let him get away with this, are you?" Evalycer asked in disbelief.

"I am for now," he said softly, looking at his sister.

"I'll be okay, Jory," Maryllia said, her voice trembling.

Jory sighed. He didn't want to leave his sister behind, but he didn't have a choice at the moment. He knew his sister was capable and determined. He motioned for his group to fall back to the ships.

"We'll let your sister go as soon as we're done with her," Keedu said, smirking.

Jory didn't like how Keedu looked as he said that, and started toward him. Tobias grabbed his arm and stopped him.

"That won't help anything, Jory," Tobias said.

With a look of loathing toward Keedu, Jory let Tobias pull him to their fighter. Evalycer got into the *Noble* with Fletcher and Yates, and they flew out of the hangar without any complications.

The flight home was silent. Even Evalycer, normally talkative, was quiet. The rescue hadn't gone quite as planned. They got two of the hostages, but the one Jory most wanted—his sister—remained behind.

When they arrived back at the base, Jory stormed off the fighter and paced angrily around until the *Noble* crew came over.

"We almost had them all," Jory said. "How did they get Maryllia?"

"I don't know," Evalycer said gently. "She probably didn't have much of a chance, being that close to Sayzan in the first place."

Jory couldn't say anything. While the others thought it was a partially successful mission, in Jory's mind it was a complete failure since they didn't get everyone back.

"We need to go see General Frey, for debriefing," he said hoarsely. "You and Aiden, too," he said, looking at Evalycer.

"You need to go see the doctor," she told him, looking at his shoulder.

"I will afterwards," he said, and he followed the others to General Frey's office.

After the debriefing, Jory went to the medical bay. The doctor looked at the wound, then washed it, applied a medication, and covered it with a bandage.

"It should be healed by tomorrow," the doctor said.

"Thanks, Doc," Jory said.

He left the medical bay and started back to the control room, but stopped short of going in. He didn't want to go in there and face his parents. His parents wouldn't blame him, but he blamed himself. He turned and headed to the officer's lounge for a quiet drink. Jory walked in and saw Tobias and Evalycer sitting at a table. He wanted to turn around and leave, but they had seen him and motioned him over to their table.

"Hey," Tobias said as Jory sat down.

Jory didn't say anything. He signaled the server and she brought over his usual Ennek scotch. He quickly tossed that back, and set the glass down harder than he intended.

"We'll get her back," Evalycer said confidently. "She'll be okay in the meantime."

"Do you know that for sure?" he finally said, looking sharply at her.

"They treated us all right while we were there," she said. "I have no reason to think they won't continue. They need her to teach them to use their abilities."

The server brought over another drink for Jory, who stared into the amber liquid. He'd figure out a way to get his sister out of there.

Chapter Seventeen

Maryllia sat in the room, now all hers, and looked out the windows into the brown haze. She knew Jory and the crew would nearly be back home by now. Jory would take her being left behind there hard, but that would also make him more determined to get her back. Her brother didn't take failure well, and that's what made him dangerous in these kind of situations.

In the meantime, she needed to try to figure out a way to get out of there. Her abilities would diminish soon, but she still had her skills. She decided she'd have to work with Keedu and his men, to help them learn to control their abilities once they drank the Elixir. She would have to convince Keedu that she needed to drink the Elixir in order to teach them and help them, which wasn't a lie. There'd be no way she could even attempt to teach them without drinking the Elixir.

The rumble in her stomach reminded Maryllia that she needed to eat. She went to the food dispenser and asked for some meat and fruit. A moment later a plate appeared, filled with those items. She took a bottle of water from the refrigerator and sat down to eat. She missed having someone there to talk to.

An hour passed, and Sayzan came to take Maryllia to the conference room for the first lesson. He didn't bother putting the restraints on her, as he knew she could hurt him or anyone else with her abilities. Her abilities were starting to fade, but she wasn't about to give him that information.

Once in the conference room, she sat across from Keedu. Sayzan sat next to him, as well as a few other members of Keedu's clan.

"So," he started. "I've brought you here so you can instruct us on how to use our abilities with the Elixir."

"In order for me to help you," Maryllia said. "I'm going to have to drink it as well."

"What makes you think I'll let you do that?"

"I have to have *my* abilities in order to see what abilities you have. If you have mind reading abilities, for example, I can't help you if I can't read your mind."

Keedu considered that for a few moments. She could see him debating in his head. He finally spoke with Sayzan and another member. After much arguing and talking, they finally came to an agreement. "Very well," Keedu said. "But we're going to put the restraints on you. We need to be able to control you, too."

"Fine," Maryllia said curtly. Sayzan came over and put the restraints on her wrists, then attached them to the chair. She could still use her hands, but couldn't leave the chair.

One of the men brought out a case of the Elixir. He gave one can to everyone, including Maryllia. They drank it quickly and waited.

"I don't feel anything happening," Keedu remarked.

"Since it's your first time, it will take a while," Maryllia told him. "You'll start to feel something in about fifteen minutes to an hour."

Once that time had passed, Maryllia noticed the men's faces. Most of them had a surprised looked on their face, a sudden realization of things they could do.

"I think I can read Sayzan's mind," Keedu said.

"You probably won't be able to read it clearly. You'll get bits and pieces of thoughts. It will become more clear after a couple of days."

Maryllia also noticed things jumping around in the room, an indication of telekinesis. She didn't know who was doing it, figuring it was all of them.

"The effects of the Elixir will last about twelve hours for you," she told them. "Once you start drinking it on a regular basis, which I sincerely hope you don't, you won't have a drop in the mornings. If you go all day without drinking it, you will lose your abilities by the end of the day."

By the end of the session, Maryllia noticed quite a few abilities surfacing in the men. Almost all of the men had strength ability, some had telekinesis, and only a handful of them had mind reading or seeing into the future. Unfortunately, Keedu turned out to have almost all abilities, since he seemed the most genetically-inclined of all of them, with his intelligence and physical traits. It frightened her to watch as his abilities formed. He had bone-crushing strength, and he learned to control his telekinesis ability alarmingly fast. She watched as Keedu used his ability on one of the slower men there, making him flinch in pain as he attempted to use the same infliction on him as she'd used on Keedu. He was only able to make the pain last for a moment. They also seemed to become more aggressive. Keedu wasn't a patient man to start with, but his lack of patience became more apparent as the Elixir took effect. She saw similar issues with some of the others as well.

In order to keep herself safe, Maryllia had to direct them on how to use their abilities, but only gave them the bare minimum for the time being. She wasn't going to help them get control of their abilities any faster than they already seemed to be doing.

"We'll take you back to your room now," Keedu told her. "We'll have another session tomorrow afternoon."

Once back in her room, Maryllia tried to think of a way to avoid teaching them more. She knew that they would drink the Elixir anyway, so what could she do to thwart their progress?

***

Jory listened to all the ideas being discussed at the table. They were all good ideas, but once they talked out how to do it, it still came down to the repulsor beam the Gantians used. Once they saw the ships coming in, they'd use it to keep them away.

"We need a ship with a cloaking device," Jory said.

"I've got one," came a voice from the doorway.

Evalycer stood there, hands on her hips, fuming.

"You do?" Jory asked.

"Yes," she said as she lowered her hands and walked slowly into the room. "And if I'd been in on this little confab, you'd have known this earlier."

"What have you got?" the general asked.

"It's a beat-up clunker, but it runs well," she started, softening her attitude. "It will fit right in with the ships coming and going from Ganta Zay."

"Tobias and I go in as traders," Jory said, thinking out loud. "We can go in with the rest of the ships and …"

"I'm going, too," Evalycer interrupted.

"What makes you think I'd let you come with us?" Jory asked.

"My ship, my rules," she shrugged. "Besides, I know where they're keeping Maryllia, I know a little about the place. You *need* me to come with you."

"You'd be willing to risk being captured again to rescue Maryllia?" Jory asked.

"Yes. Why wouldn't I?"

"I just thought you'd have had your fill of that place."

"The more people working to get her out of there, the better," Evalycer said.

The general continued. "We have the way to go in and get her out," he said. "Now we need to figure out a way to stop Lieutenant Vance giving them lessons. In the meantime, get your team together and get your plan ready. We'll execute it as soon as everything is in place."

Jory knew he wanted Tobias on the team, and Evalycer, since she was correct that they would need her knowledge of the building they'd all been held in. He'd get Fletcher and Yates to come as well.

Jory called everyone together to go over the plan. They'd need to dress in civilian clothing, but they'd take their service weapons with them.

"We'll come around Ganta Zay from the opposite direction, to throw off any trackers," Jory stated. "Then we'll fall in with the rest of the traffic going to Ganta Zay and hopefully we can find a place to land without causing any suspicions."

"I'll work on finding out what I can about Ganta Zay," Evalycer said. "I know some people who know that area."

"Good. Fletcher, you and Yates can get the weapons in order. We'll need to look like traders, but also like criminals, too. Anything you can think of that we might need to get Maryllia out."

"Will do," Fletcher replied.

"Tobi and I will go over the ship and make sure everything is working and familiarize ourselves with it. Any questions?"

No one said anything.

"We'll meet back here tomorrow morning at 0500."

Fletcher and Yates went to the weapons station while Evalycer took Jory and Tobias across the city to the Star Shot Spaceport where she had stored her ship. When they got there, Evalycer spoke to the man in the office in a language Jory didn't know. The man nodded his head, and led the three of them down a dark corridor to a dim hangar bay. The ship was as she described: run-down, beat up, and dirty. Evalycer shook the man's hand and he left them.

"What language was that?" Jory asked. "I know pretty much every language on Darantha, and that's not a local language."

"It's Torplazi, a language used on Ennek, where I was born. It's an old language that not many people know." She walked toward the ship. "For some reason, he hates using Standard. Thinks it demeans our ancestors."

"You certainly are full of surprises," Jory said.

Evalycer opened the hatch and lowered the ladder to enter the ship. Jory and Tobias followed. The inside of the ship wasn't any better than the outside of it. Evalycer saw the men looking in disbelief at the ship. "She runs better than she looks," she assured them.

"I hope so," Jory said, walking over to the pilot's console. Though it looked a bit beat up, the console was top of the line. Tobias looked around the cockpit, and noticed that it was all modern equipment.

"I fitted it with a cloaking device a few years ago," Evalycer said. "I needed it for some runs I had to do past Ornocto."

Evalycer showed Jory and Tobias everything on the ship, and after only a short time, they understood how the ship worked.

"I'll be piloting it, of course," said Evalycer. "But I need both of you to know the ins and outs of this ship. Shall we take her for a spin around the planet? We need to take it to the base, anyway."

Evalycer closed the hatch and she and Jory got into the pilot seats, with Tobias looking on from behind them. They went over the pre-flight list and were soon airborne. Evalycer expertly maneuvered the ship out of the hangar, then together they eased the thrusters and began circling Darantha. After one orbit around, Evalycer let Jory take the pilot's controls and Tobias the co-pilot's. They did some maneuvers to test out what the ship could do, though unless things got complicated, they'd be flying in normally.

Jory flew to the base and requested to land in the hangar bay. The technician gave them clearance and he set the ship down near their fighter ship.

"Well done," Evalycer said. "You two catch on quick."

"It wasn't *that* hard," Jory said, smiling.

"I'm going to get to work on finding out about Ganta Zay," Evalycer said. "I'll see you all tomorrow morning."

***

Evalycer found a ride back to Star Shot Spaceport to find the man she spoke to earlier. The man, Gareth, was the owner of the hangar who also had connections to traders and other less-than-reputable people.

"You're back so soon?" Gareth asked in Torplazi as Evalycer walked in.

"I need your help," she said, sitting in the chair opposite his desk. "What can you tell me about Ganta Zay and the Gantians?"

Two hours later, Evalycer had a better understanding of the Gantians and their planet. Or so she hoped. It would have to be enough, since they were leaving the next morning to try to free Maryllia.

Chapter Eighteen

At 0500 there was only a minimal amount of personnel in the command center when Jory arrived. Eager to get the rescue mission going, he'd gotten to the base just a little before the agreed-upon time to go over the ship once more. Tobias came in a few minutes later, followed by Evalycer, Yates, and Fletcher. They met in a small conference room briefly to go over what Evalycer had learned.

"We all know that they are pirates or criminals of some sort," Evalycer started. "They don't care who they hurt to get what they want. They are aggressive by nature, so they tend to act first, then maybe ask questions later. Most of the time, they don't ask."

"Friendly bunch," Yates remarked.

"They will keep Maryllia alive as long as she keeps doing what they want her to do. If she decides to stop teaching them, they will kill her."

"Damn it," Jory said. "I wish I could somehow tell her to keep doing what she's doing so they don't hurt her."

"We need to get there as fast as we can," Evalycer told him. "If she tries to stop teaching them, they may 'persuade' her to keep teaching them. After that…"

Jory knew the urgency to get her out. "Is everyone ready?" he asked.

Everyone answered in the affirmative.

"Tobi and I will check in with General Frey, then we'll go."

"Don't do anything unnecessary," General Frey said when Jory and Tobias met with him in the office. "Go in, get her out, come home. We all know it won't be that easy, but just stay focused on the mission. Nothing else matters. We don't have to worry about the Elixir they've hijacked."

"Yes, sir," Jory said.

They found Evalycer checking over the ship one more time before they were to leave.

"Everything okay?" Jory asked.

"Yep," she said.

Evalycer got into the pilot's seat, and Jory in the co-pilot's seat. The rest of the crew took their seats just behind the cockpit, and all had headsets to communicate with each other. Jory, Tobias, Fletcher, and Yates had ditched their RPF uniforms for a more rugged look. Dressed in dark brown pants with many pockets, torn khaki green shirt, leather jacket, and his weapons belt, Jory hoped he looked the part of a criminal. The others were dressed in a similar fashion. Evalycer always dressed the part.

They received permission to leave. Evalycer pushed buttons to start the engines as Jory checked the read-outs. Once the engines came online, Evalycer and Jory pushed the controllers forward and the ship lurched forward, then smoothed out as they left the hangar bay. As they cleared the planet's gravity, they shot into light speed, headed toward Ganta Zay.

It took them longer to reach the asteroid belt going in that direction, and brought them much nearer to Ganta Zay. Evalycer hit the button to bring them back to sub-light speed and contacted the security escort. Once through the asteroid belt, Evalycer engaged the cloaking device in case the Gantians were monitoring the area. They didn't want to be seen coming through the asteroid belt.

***

Maryllia awoke that morning dreading to start the day. She knew that she would again be teaching Keedu and his cronies how to use their abilities from the Elixir. It made her sick thinking about teaching them, but how could she get around it? If she refused to teach them, who knew what they'd do to her. They'd already shown they weren't a stable race.

She went into the bathroom to shower, trying to work out some way to avoid teaching them. The hot water relaxed her so she could think more clearly.

After she dried and dressed, Maryllia ordered her breakfast and took a water from the refrigerator. She had come up with a plan while showering and hoped it would work. She'd have to implement it quickly, but depending on when they came for her, she may not have full use of her abilities.

Fortunately she didn't have to wait long. Sayzan came for her just as she finished her meal. As they walked down the corridor, Maryllia found it fairly easy to probe Sayzan's mind, since the effects of the Elixir he'd drunk had already worn off. She searched for any weakness or uncertainty he might have—anything she could use against him as they learned to use their abilities.

Maryllia found that Sayzan didn't like being second in command. Keedu always bullied him or made him do the "dirty work" for him. She'd save that bit of information for later. They arrived at the conference room a moment later. She started working quickly on Keedu once she entered the room. She didn't find much to work with on him. He was confident in his position, but he did have some reservations with some of his crew. They weren't performing up to his standards. How could she use this information to her advantage?

"Welcome back," Keedu was saying. She came out of her thoughts and focused on him. "I hope you had a good nights' sleep?"

"It would have been better if I'd been in my own bed," she said.

"How soon you get to go back depends on how much we accomplish in the next couple of days," he told her.

Sayzan had brought out cans of Elixir as they'd been speaking. Maryllia sat in a chair and he gave her a can of Elixir to drink before putting on the restraints.

"It will take about fifteen to thirty minutes for the Elixir to take effect," Maryllia reminded them.

After they all drank their Elixir, Maryllia started reading their minds. She was going to find something to use against them somehow, even if she had to exaggerate the truth.

"Today we're going to practice reading each other's minds," she told them. "Not all of you will be able to do it, but we'll figure out who can as we go along." She already knew that Keedu could read minds, since he had already started to at the last session.

The men started acquiring their abilities about half an hour later. Items started to dance around on the desk. Maryllia delved into Sayzan's mind again and saw that he became more agitated as the Elixir took effect. In fact, all of them were becoming belligerent.

"Why can't I control these abilities?" Keedu demanded.

"Like I said yesterday, it will take some time. It takes about a week for your abilities to fully form and for you to take some kind of control over them," Maryllia replied. "We're going to focus on mind-reading today. I want all of you to sit down and calm your mind."

The men sat down and she waited for all of them to calm their thoughts. It was hard for Keedu and Sayzan to do it, being the most aggressive men in the room. As they sat, she tried to again read their minds to find something to use against them. She'd start with who she hoped was the weaker of the two.

"Sayzan, I want you to concentrate on Keedu. Relax your mind as you try to read his. I'm going to read his mind as well to see if what you see is correct."

"You're not probing my mind," Keedu said, looking at Maryllia.

"I could have done so at any time, Keedu," Maryllia replied. "Your thoughts are not safe in your head with me around. Why do you think I'm the Lead Interrogator?"

Maryllia could see that Keedu hadn't thought of that. Keedu slowly nodded his head for Sayzan and Maryllia to continue. Sayzan looked at Keedu, staring into his eyes. Maryllia did the same. She could see how much Keedu hated having her read his mind. She came across some dark spots, figuring those were things he didn't want her to know.

He caught on to that part quickly, she thought.

Sayzan didn't spend much time on reading Keedu's mind. She knew it was a hard ability to do well.

"Keedu really despises you," Sayzan said, smiling.

"That much I already knew," Maryllia said. "But yes, I saw that as well. What else?"

"I couldn't see much else. There were blank spots that I couldn't see."

"You can get into those dark places if you try hard enough. Try again."

Sayzan stared at Keedu again as he tried to get through the dark spots. Maryllia knew that Sayzan didn't yet have the skills to do it, but it gave her time to dig through Keedu's mind to find out what he was hiding.

She saw that even though Sayzan was his second-in-command, Keedu didn't trust him very much. She also saw that they had some sort of weapon that rendered engines and weapons useless.

"I can't see anything else," Sayzan said angrily. Maryllia switched briefly to Sayzan's mind, and saw how frustrated he was that Keedu hid things from him.

"It will take practice." She turned to Keedu. "Keedu, I want you to do that same with Sayzan."

What Maryllia did next had only been done a few times. While Keedu read Sayzan's mind, Maryllia pulled Sayzan's thoughts up to the front to make them easier to read. She wanted to make sure that Keedu saw those thoughts Sayzan had regarding Keedu and how he was treated. Since Keedu was just learning to read minds, Maryllia doubted that he'd be able to read her mind and Sayzan's at the same time.

Keedu suddenly jumped out of his chair. "You want to take over the planet?" he growled.

"I never thought that!" Sayzan exclaimed.

"Then what did I just see?" he turned to Maryllia. "You saw it, didn't you?"

"I did," Maryllia replied calmly.

"And, you don't trust me because you think I'm keeping things from you? That's why you couldn't read my thoughts?" Keedu scowled.

"I should know everything you know, as I'm your second-in-command! If you don't trust me, how can I trust you?"

Keedu pulled out his knife and lunged at Sayzan. Sayzan side-stepped out of the way, pushing the hand with the blade out of the way. They both threw punches, and Maryllia heard Keedu's fist connect with Sayzan's jaw. Sayzan spit blood from his mouth, and aimed a kick at Keedu's stomach, knocking him back, but not down.

Maryllia hadn't predicted this. She was restrained in the chair and if things got more violent, she could get hurt. She used her ability to momentarily bring pain to both of the men. They stopped fighting and doubled over. But as quickly as the pain came, it was gone again.

"You both need to calm down," Maryllia shouted.

Both men looked over to her, panting heavily.

"These lessons are over for today," she told them firmly. "And I'm not going to teach you anything else until you both work out your problems. This isn't my problem."

Keedu sent his men out of the room. He walked over to Maryllia and stood in front of her. He bent down, bringing his face even with hers, tapping his knife on her knees. "You will continue these lessons when I say you will," he said calmly, but Maryllia knew he was anything but calm. He took the restraints off of her, pulled her roughly from her chair, and took her back to her room himself.

"I will summon you later to continue the lesson once everyone has had time to calm down." She heard him lock the door and walk away.

Her plan would only work once. She couldn't do that same thing again. She had to come up with something else to prevent the lessons. In their agitated state, she wondered if they would calm down enough that day to continue.

Since the building wasn't shielded, she could still read their minds. Neither one trusted the other one and they were angry with each other. Keedu wasn't speaking to Sayzan even though Sayzan tried pleading with him to listen. Keedu didn't like people who begged, either, and sent Sayzan out of the room.

Mission accomplished.

***

"We're coming up on the traffic pattern to Ganta Zay," Evalycer said. "We'll fly above it, decloak, and settle into the traffic with the rest of the ships."

Evalycer maneuvered the ship above the planet traffic, and as they decloaked, they flew into the traffic. None of the other pilots around them seemed to notice anything.

"We'll be on Ganta Zay in about ten minutes," Jory told the rest of the crew.

Five minutes out, everyone started to check their weapons. Evalycer scanned the computer for a safe place to land just outside the city. As they approached the planet, the air around them became darker and more dense.

"We're going to have to fly on instruments and ability," Evalycer remarked.

"This is horrendous," Tobias said. "How can anyone survive in this?"

"That's why they wear masks outside and have to trade for food," Jory said. "They can't survive otherwise."

"It's a good place to hide for those who want to hide," Evalycer remarked.

Evalycer found a small spaceport outside the city limits in which to land. As they descended, she pointed out where Maryllia was being held.

"I'm not sure what level we were held on," Evalycer told Jory. "But it was high enough to see over the city."

Evalycer contacted the spaceport for permission to land. They had concocted a story to tell in case they were asked any questions, and they had to sound convincing now.

"We're bounty hunters looking for a fugitive," Jory said.

"We don't allow extradition from here," came the reply.

"Then you may want to quarantine your people," he said. "Heavily contagious with Orex pox. Hopefully we can get to him before he sneezes on someone."

After a few moments of silence, they were allowed to land.

"You will need to quarantine this port, however," Tobias said as the man met them. "That way we can bring the fugitive in without contaminating anyone."

"W-w-we'll keep this area clear," the man stuttered.

"Excellent," Jory said. They donned their masks and set out into the putrid air.

Their head lamps barely cut through the smoggy air. Even at ground level it was difficult to see through. Everyone around them wore the same type of clothing and headgear. It made it easy for the crew to go about the city undetected.

From the intel Evalycer had received from her man at the Star Shot Spaceport, they knew which areas to avoid. Patrols watched the area, but they couldn't be everywhere at once. Jory led the crew down a side street, away from an approaching patrol. Once it passed, they had about ten minutes before the next one would come by in that area.

Evalycer pointed out which way the needed to go next. They could just make out the building from their vantage point on the street. They hurried along the street, acting like they were looking for someone every so often, in case anyone asked questions. There were a surprising number of people on the streets for the air being so bad. Luckily no one seemed to care that they were there.

The next patrol would be coming around soon, so they got off the street and went into a tavern. They pulled off their masks to breathe in the filtered air inside, found a table in the corner and a girl came over to take their drink order. She left for a few minutes and came back with their drinks.

"Once we get to the building," Jory started. "We'll need to hurry. Are you sure you can remember where the room is?"

"Not a hundred percent sure, but when they brought us down when you came to rescue us, they didn't put a blindfold on us. I think we were eight floors up."

"Maybe you should try and contact her," Tobias said. "Let her know we're coming."

Using his mind-reading ability, Jory did his best to concentrate on Maryllia. The bar was noisy, but he closed his eyes and cleared his head of everything except for rescuing his sister. He could almost feel Maryllia's presence there. He let her know, he hoped, that they were coming to rescue her and were there in the city.

Chapter Nineteen

We're coming!

Maryllia saw that loud and clear in her mind. She closed her eyes and relaxed to try to see if this was a true statement, that Jory really was on his way to rescue her. *In the city nearby. Be prepared to leave.*

Maryllia opened her eyes and smiled with relief. Her brother had returned and she'd be freed soon. She had to let him know her location, where she might be later, and that the Gantians had become more hostile as the Elixir took effect. She closed her eyes again to contact Jory and thought she was successful in sending her message to him.

Once she finished, she cleared her mind. Maryllia knew that Keedu was a strong mind reader; he'd see that right away. Just as she was an expert at reading people's minds, she was also good at hiding things.

She knew she'd be called upon again to teach them to use their abilities later that day and hoped that the Gantians had calmed down. She'd refuse to teach them if they weren't calm.

***

Keedu paced around his office, thinking. *How dare Sayzan defy me!* He'd known that Sayzan wanted to be in command, but he was grooming Sayzan to do so—someday. Sayzan wanted the power now. *Well, he's not going to get it now, and he may not get it at all.* He called Sayzan into his office, along with a security guard.

"I will not stand by and be disrespected," Keedu told his subordinate.

"And neither will I," Sayzan replied. "I can do this job as well as you can. Maybe better."

Keedu came around his desk to face Sayzan. "You think so? Try and take this knife from me. Go on," he prodded when Sayzan seemed to hesitate.

Sayzan looked at the knife for a moment, then made a move to retrieve it. Keedu swiftly made Sayzan double over in pain.

"I will not be disrespected," Keedu said again, emphasizing each word.

Sayzan nodded, and the pain stopped.

"Go get our teacher again. It's time to continue the lessons."

"Yes, sir," Sayzan said, making sure to be respectful, even if he didn't feel it.

***

The knock on the door startled Maryllia. She stuffed the last piece of bread into her mouth and turned toward the door. It opened and Sayzan stood there, waiting for her.

"Already?" she asked.

Sayzan didn't reply, but his steely stare told her to keep quiet. She walked out into the corridor and Sayzan took her by the arm and dragged her to the elevator to take her back down to the conference room. Maryllia read Sayzan's mind as they descended, and found that he and Keedu had argued. That would account for his surly demeanor.

Keedu was seated at his desk. There were less men there than earlier. Sayzan put Maryllia roughly into the chair and put the restraints on.

"Do not hurt our teacher, Sayzan," Keedu said without looking up. He finished what he was working on then looked up at Maryllia.

"Where are the others?' Maryllia asked.

"I think it's better that we do this in smaller groups," Keedu told her. "Too many things can go wrong with more people. We will learn what we can, then teach the others ourselves."

Maryllia started teaching them how to read minds again. This time, however, she had Keedu watch and observe instead of participate. She knew he already could read minds. He learned everything rapidly. Sayzan and the other men took a little more time. With each attempt, they grew more frustrated and anxious, feeling like they weren't living up to what Keedu wanted.

"I don't care what anyone thinks," Maryllia told them all. "It takes time to learn to use the abilities well. You can fly by the seat of your pants and do it haphazardly, but you won't be doing it correctly. Learning to read someone's mind is tricky to do well. You need to learn to read what others don't want you to see," she said, looking at Keedu.

"You're saying that even if someone hides their thoughts, they can be read?" Keedu asked gruffly.

"Yes," Maryllia said. "If the person reading minds is skilled enough."

"So what's the point of learning to hide your thoughts if they can be read anyway?" Keedu asked, his anger rising.

"Only someone who has exceptional skills at mind-reading can do it."

"Like you."

"Yes. It takes months of practice." She hoped that placing that information into Keedu's mind would keep him from trying to probe her mind or anyone else's to find any hidden thoughts.

"So even if Sayzan is hiding something from me, I can find it eventually," he said, looking at Sayzan. Sayzan stood up to challenge Keedu. Once again Keedu used his ability to bring momentary pain to Sayzan, and he backed down.

As the lesson continued, Keedu and Sayzan constantly bickered. Mostly it was Keedu teaching Sayzan his place, and Sayzan growing more agitated by his lack of control over his abilities. It wasn't lack of control, however, it was that Keedu had mastered it so quickly. Keedu held them all to his standard, even with Maryllia telling them it was unusual and not the norm.

Maryllia was relieved when Keedu announced they were done for the day. Sayzan took her back to her room and locked the door.

***

"Let's get going," Jory said, tossing back his drink. Everyone pulled their masks back on as they headed outside again. Twilight was setting upon the city, which made it easier for the group to hide in the shadows and smog. They left the lights on their headgear off, so they could stay as inconspicuous as possible the closer they got to the building.

It took them half an hour to get across the city to the building where Maryllia was being held. Once they got near, they looked for ways to get inside. They knew where the hanger bay was, which was an option. Going through the offices made less sense, as there would surely be people there, even at that hour, since that was also a residence.

They decided the hangar bay was the best option. Jory led the way, with Evalycer behind him, telling him where to go. The group got to the open hangar doors, but bright lights illuminated the doorway.

"We'll have to go in one at a time," Jory said. "The rest of us will cover you until we're all in."

They agreed. Tobias went in first. He made sure that the guards were otherwise occupied before he ran inside and found cover behind some containers. Next was Yates, followed by Evalycer. The crew inside then covered Fletcher and Jory as they came inside.

Once inside, it was easy to stay under cover in the shadows of the ships and behind the containers along the walls. They moved

156

slowly and carefully along the walls, using Evalycer's guidance. They found a spot behind some barrels in a corner to stop and assess what they needed to do next.

"I don't know if they left guards outside the door or not," Evalycer told them. "They always had about four guards to escort us everywhere. We just assumed they did and never tried to escape. We could've easily just unlocked the door, but not knowing what was outside the door, and with Aiden freaking out..."

"We could meet some resistance once we find which floor she's on," Jory said.

"But, they will most likely either not have the Elixir in their system, or not know how to control whatever abilities they have."

"Works to our advantage," Tobias said.

Jory cleared his mind to try to reach out to find where Maryllia was being held. Not knowing the layout of the building made it harder for Jory to do so. With Evalycer's guidance, he was able to find out how to get into the residential part of the building.

"Sorry it's not more," Evalycer said.

"It's helpful," Jory told her.

A loud creaking and scraping noise echoed through the hangar bay. Jory quickly turned to see the hangar bay doors being shut for the night. He slammed his fist into a crate. Luckily, it gave way slightly.

"There goes our best way out," Fletcher said.

"We'll have to find another way," Jory said, shaking his hand out.

Once the doors were closed, most of the guards left the area, leaving only a handful for the night duties.

Jory nodded, and they all crept along the wall to the doorway opposite them. Tobias looked out the doorway and saw no one in the corridor. Jory led the way, stopping short of the intersecting hallway. Jory positioned himself on one side, Evalycer on the other, using their abilities to check down each end to make sure the coast was clear.

The crew went down the left corridor to the elevators, but before they could push the button to call the elevator, someone came around the corner at the end of the corridor.

"Who are you?" the guard demanded, drawing his weapon and pointing it at the group.

"We're looking for the prisoner," Jory said. "We were told to move her to another floor."

"I'll have to check that out," the guard said, pulling out his communicator.

The guard suddenly dropped to the floor, unconscious.

"Nice work, whoever that was," Jory said, turning to face the others.

"You're welcome," Evalycer said. "We don't have time to deal with these idiots."

Tobias punched the button for the elevator, and they waited only a few moments for it to arrive. Luckily, the car was empty. Jory hit the button for the eighth floor. The doors shut quickly and the car started to ascend.

The car stopped on the desired floor. As the doors slid open, the group aimed their weapons outward, expecting to see someone there. The corridor was empty ahead of them. Jory quickly looked around the doors to the left and right. Seeing no one, he motioned for them all to follow him.

They moved slowly down the corridor, looking ahead with their abilities for any guards or others that may be on the floor. Jory could feel Maryllia's presence as they got nearer her room.

"It's down that hallway," Evalycer whispered to Jory, motioning down the left corridor. They both peeked around the corner and saw two armed guards outside Maryllia's room. Jory held up two fingers to the others behind him. They got their weapons ready, and they ran out into the corridor toward the guards. One of the guards grabbed his communicator as the other aimed his weapon. Jory shot the guard with the communicator in the shoulder, as Evalycer shot the other one dead. Tobias jammed his foot into the fallen guard's face, rendering him unconscious.

Fletcher unlocked the door as the others kept a look around. The door opened and Maryllia stood in the middle of the room, surprised yet happy to see them.

"Jory!" she exclaimed. Jory rushed in and embraced his sister quickly.

"Are you all right?" he asked her.

"I'm fine," she said. "We need to get out of here, fast. The Gantians are getting more aggressive each time they drink the Elixir. I don't know what they'd do if they found us escaping."

Tobias gave Maryllia a weapon and a mask to wear for when they left the building. Jory looked out into the corridor before they took off down the way they came. Checking ahead with their abilities, they found the corridors clear. They arrived at the elevators and saw that it was on its way back up again.

"Shit!" Jory said.

"They're probably coming to get me to teach them another lesson," Maryllia suggested.

They went back down the corridor and down the opposite way they had come. They found a storage room that was unlocked. They ran in and shut the door, leaving it open just enough to see which way the new group went. They went straight to Maryllia's room. Once they saw the guards on the floor, the door open and Maryllia gone, one of the men made a call on his communicator and immediately an alarm sounded.

"We'll have to find another way out," Evalycer said. She closed her eyes to see if there were any other ways off that floor. Maryllia did the same.

"Well?" Jory asked impatiently. He wanted to get out of there as soon as possible.

"There is a stairwell at the end of the corridor," Maryllia said. Evalycer nodded in agreement. "It will take us down to the second floor. I don't know why it stops there."

"It'll have to do," Jory said. "Let's go."

Tobias looked out into the corridor and saw only one guard standing by Maryllia's room. He stood watching the guard as the others ran toward the door at the end of the corridor. The guard turned and raised his weapon, but Tobias used his ability to render him unconscious before the guard got a shot off.

The group ran down the stairs, stopping before each floor to make sure no one was coming up before continuing. They got to the second floor landing. There indeed was nowhere to go except out the door.

Jory pulled the door and found it was locked. He nodded his head toward the door and heard a soft *click*, indicating it was now unlocked. He opened the door just a crack, to see where they had ended up. It looked to be a control room. There were a few men and women in there, but most had left to heed the alarm of the escaped hostage.

"There are about twenty people left," Jory said.

"But those people don't have abilities like we do," Evalycer reminded him.

Jory looked out across the room and saw another door. He closed his eyes to see if they led to a stairway down to the hangar bay. It did.

"We have to head for that door over there," Jory told them, pointing across the room. "Those stairs will lead us to the hangar bay."

"How do we get out of there once we get there?" Yates asked. "They closed the hangar doors."

"There's got to be another door to the outside somewhere," Jory said.

"We'll find it," Evalycer said, irritated. "I just want to get the hell out of here."

Jory pulled the door open and they ran across the room. They were halfway to the door before anyone noticed them. At first no one said or did anything, but they noticed Maryllia wasn't dressed like the others.

"Look! Over there!" a woman shouted. Several people drew their weapons as others hit the floor to get out of the way.

The rescue group returned fire, hitting their marks as they made their way across the room. Jory got to the door first. He held it open as Evalycer came up and covered the others as they entered through the door. As Maryllia got through the doorway, laser fire hit her right leg. She screamed as she fell inside the doorway as both Jory and Evalycer returned fire, hitting the man who shot Maryllia. Evalycer scrambled inside and Jory let the door close. He aimed his weapon at the lock and melted the metal so they couldn't open the door to follow.

"Are you okay?" Jory asked, his face ashen.

Tobias and Yates were working on Maryllia's wound. Tobias sprinkled a pain medication on it and Yates got ready to bind the wound.

"I'm okay," Maryllia said, her teeth clenched in pain.

"Can you walk?"

"I'm going to have to," she said. "You can't carry me. I'll be fine," she said when she saw Jory's worried face.

When Yates finished binding Maryllia's leg, the group started down the stairs to the hangar bay, Maryllia limping along but keeping up. Jory knew she was in a lot of pain, but also knew she wasn't going to let anyone, especially him, know.

Once in the hangar bay, they walked quickly along the wall, staying in the shadows as much as possible, the way they had come in. Jory reached out with his abilities to find another door to lead them outside. They put on their masks as they followed Jory to the door and out, Yates half-carrying Maryllia.

Once outside, they had to get their bearings again, since they came out a different door than they went in. Jory and Tobias figured out which way they needed to go. Jory led the way, with Tobias bringing up the rear. Maryllia kept going despite the pain Jory knew she felt.

The group stopped once to let Maryllia and Yates rest. Jory told Maryllia the story of her being infected with Orex pox and that the port where the ship was kept should be quarantined.

"There shouldn't be anyone there except the proprietor," Jory said.

"Good," Maryllia said. Her face was pallid. She wasn't losing blood, but the effort to move such a long distance was taking its toll.

"We're almost there," Evalycer told her.

They started again. They had to duck down an alley as a patrol went by. There'd been a lot more activity in the streets as they made their way back, most likely due to the escape.

They saw the spaceport a block away. Maryllia found new strength as she knew the journey was nearly over. At least this part of it. They still had to get past the tractor beam.

Chapter Twenty

"How did she escape?" Keedu demanded.

"There's no way she could've escaped," Sayzan said. "She most likely was rescued by the RPF, meaning her brother, Prince Jordan."

Keedu paced the floor, then lunged at his desk and turned it over. The desk wasn't lightweight; it was made from a heavy wood. Another ability had formed—strength.

"We have men looking for them," Sayzan told him.

"Is the tractor beam ready?" Keedu asked, looking toward the control panel.

"It's ready, sir," said the technician.

Keedu stood behind the technician and watched as they scanned for the ship. They had no idea what they were looking for. With so much activity and traffic going in and out of the planet, they'd have a hard time finding it.

***

The crew ran into the spaceport, Yates nearly dragging Maryllia inside. Her leg had become immobile and the pain nearly excruciating. As promised, the area where they had landed was deserted. Jory hit the button to open the hatch, and they climbed inside. Jory took one last look around to make sure no one had seen them, then ducked inside and closed the hatch.

Yates and Jory lifted Maryllia onto a table in the back. She groaned loudly, and pulled off her mask. "I don't know what they hit me with," Maryllia said. "But it hurts like hell."

Her face was covered in sweat and red from the exertion. Jory covered her with a blanket and looked at her wound.

"Jory, don't you need to get us out of here?" she said with effort.

"Tobi can co-pilot this thing with Evalycer," he said. "You're my priority right now."

They felt the ship rise and move forward. Jory grabbed the side of the table to keep from falling, then the flight smoothed out. He grabbed a headset so he could communicate with the cockpit.

"Hey," Jory said. "I think if we just fall back into the traffic, we should be okay."

"That's what I'm hoping," Evalycer said. "Because I've got no more tricks to evade them from here."

"Copy that." He turned back to Maryllia. "I'm sorry, but we have to go the long way around Ganta Zay to get back home."

"It's okay," Maryllia whispered. "I'm just glad to be out of there."

Evalycer jumped right into the traffic pattern from Ganta Zay. She hoped with all the ships leaving the spaceports, Keedu wouldn't know which one was theirs.

***

"I'm having trouble finding them, sir," the technician said. "They must've come in an unmarked ship, not an RPF ship."

Keedu screamed in frustration, slamming his fists onto the top of the console, nearly crushing it. The technician jumped out of his chair, stumbling over another chair to get out of the way. Keedu stormed from the room, Sayzan following at a distance.

Keedu went into his office, his desk still laying on its side. Keedu looked at Sayzan and Sayzan snapped his fingers and two guards picked up the desk and put back into position. They started to pick up the items scattered on the floor, but Keedu waved them off. He sat in his chair, the veins in his head pulsing.

"What do you want to do?" Sayzan asked.

Keedu said nothing. Sayzan wasn't sure if Keedu had heard him, and was about to repeat his statement. Keedu finally roused and looked at Sayzan.

"How dare you want to defy me and my orders."

"What are you talking about? I haven't defied anyone," Sayzan replied angrily.

"What I read in your thoughts earlier. You want to take over my position."

"I may want to someday, but not now. That woman is the Lead Interrogator in the RPF. She probably put those ideas in my head for you to see."

Keedu thought about that. He hadn't realized how much power the Elixir could give someone. Was it possible to plant ideas and thoughts into another person's mind as well as read minds? Knowing how good the princess was at her job, it most likely was possible.

"We're going to make her pay for causing trouble with us," Keedu said now. "We'll need a plan to get her back."

***

The trip around Ganta Zay was excruciatingly slow, or so it seemed. Jory wanted to be home, but they had to keep the pretense of being just another supply ship. As they entered Ganta Zay's airspace, Evalycer ascended above the traffic and cloaked the ship.

"Should only be another half-hour until we get to the asteroid belt," Evalycer said. "Then we can go light-speed to Darantha."

"Good," Jory said into the headset. "Maryllia doesn't look so good."

Evalycer joined Jory in the back a moment later. "What's wrong?"

"I don't think this was an ordinary laser hit," Jory said quietly. Maryllia had fallen asleep. He carefully moved the blanket out of the way, and gently removed the binding on her leg. The wound had turned a bright yellow, but the skin around it was black. "She can't move her leg at all."

"Damn it," Evalycer said. "I thought I had found out everything about the Gantians. I've never heard about these weapons." She went to the computer and ran a search on the Gantian's weapons.

"We're coming up on the asteroid belt," Tobias said in the headset.

"Decloak us and I'll be up there in a minute," Evalycer replied.

Evalycer studied that computer findings, looking for anything remotely similar to what happened to Maryllia. She found nothing specific regarding Ganta Zay's weapons, but did find out a little about the wound.

"It looks like it's some sort of chemical blast," Evalycer said slowly. "It's not a laser blast. 'The chemical, when used as a weapon, can immobilize the victim with a direct hit. It will continue to eat the flesh until...'" she read, trailing off, scanning ahead. "We gotta try and get that chemical out of her flesh, Jory, or it eats her flesh to the bone."

"Does it say how to do this?" Jory asked, his voice rising in pitch.

Evalycer studied the computer again. "We have to cut it out."

"What? Cut into her leg?"

"Yes. It doesn't look too bad right now, but if we wait until we get back, it will definitely be worse." She looked at Jory, who frowned. She stood up and walked over to him and put her hand on his left shoulder. "Look at the computer and see what we need and get it together. I'll be back as soon as we get through the asteroids." With that, she patted his shoulder and went to the cockpit.

Jory looked over the items they would need to do this surgery. Knife, anesthetic, bandages, something to sterilize everything. Jory asked Yates to start looking for the items as Jory quickly began to search. He had his knife with him. Yates had pain meds, though Jory wasn't sure if that would be enough to use for anesthetic. The closest thing they had to sterilize everything was a bottle of ale.

Jory felt the ship shift and knew they had entered the asteroid belt. Even with the ship's stabilizers and gravity, he still lurched from side to side every so often. The ship smoothed out and Evalycer came back.

"We're ready to go light speed," she said. "But that still gets us back to Darantha in an hour. Too long to wait." She looked at all the items they had found. "These will have to do. Wake her up. We gotta tell her what's going on."

Jory gently shook Maryllia's shoulder. She stirred and slowly opened her eyes. "Are we back?"

"No," Jory said. "We have to cut this chemical out of your leg, Lia. Otherwise you can lose part of your leg."

"Can't it wait?"

"No," Evalycer said firmly. "We have to do it now."

Maryllia nodded. "Do it."

"It's going to hurt like hell," Evalycer said.

"Okay," Maryllia replied.

Evalycer opened the bottle of ale and poured it on Jory's knife. She poured the remainder on Maryllia's leg. She winced and jerked her leg.

"Give her the pain meds now," Evalycer told Yates. "They'll give her some relief, and will be helpful once we're done."

Yates pulled out the pain medication and put two into Maryllia's mouth and held a cup of water up to her lips. She swallowed the pills down.

Jory looked at the wound. He tried to disassociate the wound from his sister, but had a hard time doing so. His hand shook as he held the knife over the wound, ready to cut. He breathed in slowly to steady himself, but his hands still shook.

"You hold her down," Evalycer told him, seeing his reaction. "I'll cut."

Jory gave his knife to Evalycer and went to the head of Maryllia's bed. He placed his hands on her shoulders and used his Strength ability to hold her down.

"I'm cutting now," Evalycer said as she made that first cut into the flesh. Maryllia flinched violently, her eyes flew open, but Jory held her down. Yates grabbed Maryllia's legs and held them as Evalycer made the cuts. Maryllia cried out in pain as each cut went deeper into her muscle. Jory tried not to look while Evalycer cut into Maryllia's leg, whispering soothing words into Maryllia's ear.

Evalycer worked rapidly but carefully, cutting a little at a time, making sure to only take out the damaged tissue. Maryllia quieted down, so either the meds were working or she was losing consciousness. Either way, they needed to hurry.

"Almost done," Evalycer said. She trimmed the skin around the wound and mopped up the blood in and around it. Jory looked and saw that wound looked much better. The yellow ooze was gone and it was just raw flesh. Evalycer packed the wound with the bandages, then wrapped a bandage around her leg. Jory slowly released Maryllia's shoulders and Yates her legs.

Maryllia's breathing returned to normal as they cleaned the blood off the table and floor. Jory took a cloth and blotted the sweat from her forehead. She opened her eyes for a moment and Jory sighed with relief.

"You doing okay?" he asked.

Maryllia nodded. "That was fun. Let's do that again sometime," she joked weakly.

"She's fine," Evalycer said, gathering up the supplies and putting them into a compartment to take care of later. She wiped her hands on a cloth and started back to the cockpit, but stopped to say, "Glad you're still with us, Lieutenant."

Maryllia slept for the rest of the flight home. Evalycer contacted the base when they were fifteen minutes away, alerting them to Maryllia's condition and to have a medical team waiting for them.

They received priority landing instructions from the base, to land nearest the medical bay. The medical team came in and got Maryllia on a gurney and took her straight into the surgical room, Jory following them.

Once they got Maryllia into the examination room, the doctor came in and looked at Maryllia's wound carefully as Jory watched from the window outside of the room. The doctor spent fifteen minutes looking at the wound, running tests, using his microscopic glasses to look into the wound. He straightened and came out to speak to Jory.

"Who took care of the wound?" the doctor asked.

"My pilot, Evalycer Nicholls," Jory told him. "I was going to but my hands were shaking."

"Well, she did an excellent job on it. She got all of the chemical out of the wound and tidied up the skin around the wound. I'd like to speak to her about it."

"I'll let her know, but I wouldn't count on talking to her," Jory laughed. "She pretty much keeps to herself."

"Please thank her for me. The princess will make a full recovery, but she'll have to stay overnight so we can monitor her healing after we apply the medication to restore her muscle and skin."

Jory shook the doctor's hand and left. As he entered the hanger bay heading to the general's office, he saw his parents walking toward him.

"How is Maryllia?" his mother asked.

"She's going to be fine," Jory told her. "The doctor said she'll make a full recovery. Evalycer did a great job cleaning out the wound."

"I want to meet her as soon as it's convenient for her," Leander said.

Jory thought how well that would go over with Evalycer. "I'll tell her," Jory said.

His parents continued to the medical bay and Jory proceeded to the general's office. The rest of the crew were already there.

"How is Lieutenant Vance?" the general asked.

Jory told them all what the doctor said, and specifically that the doctor wanted to meet Evalycer. "That ain't gonna happen," she said firmly.

"My parents also want to meet you," he told her.

Evalycer sighed. "I guess that one will have to happen. We can meet with them after the debriefing."

They spent thirty minutes going over every detail of what happened on Ganta Zay before being dismissed. Yates and Fletcher went home. Tobias went to his and Jory's office to file the report while Jory and Evalycer went to the medical bay.

Maryllia was resting comfortably in her private room with a guard at the door. The guard nodded to Jory as he approached and Jory and Evalycer went into the room.

"Mother, Father," Jory said. "This is Evalycer Nicholls. Evalycer, King Leander and Queen Arika."

"Your Majesties," Evalycer said, nodding her head politely to the both of them.

Queen Arika went over to Evalycer and hugged her. Jory could see how uncomfortable Evalycer was, as she had not expected this kind of informality from the queen.

"Thank you for what you did for Maryllia," Arika said. "I hear that she could have lost her leg if you hadn't cut the chemical out."

"I just did what I had to do, ma'am, and what Maryllia would have done for me," Evalycer said, taking a step back from the queen.

"Leander and I spoke, and we'd like to honor you with a title for helping our daughter."

Evalycer froze. When she found her voice again, she said, "That really isn't necessary, ma'am."

"We insist," King Leander said.

Evalycer stammered her thanks, gave a nod to them both, and backed out of the room. Jory followed.

"No!" she shouted to Jory. "Absolutely not. No title. That is so not me."

Jory grinned, amused at her reaction. "I'll talk to them and let them know it's not what you want."

Evalycer visibly relaxed. "Thank you."

"I'll see you later. I'm going home to my wife and a home-cooked meal."

"I'm going to find a card game somewhere," she said. "See ya later."

Evalycer hurried to her transport and left while Jory said goodbye to Tobias and headed home.

Jory found Samara working on her lessons for the Academy when he arrived home. It'd been a long eventful day, and he just wanted dinner and a shower. Samara came out of the study when she heard Jory close the door.

"How did it go?" she asked, kissing him quickly.

They sat on the sofa and he told her the story of the rescue and how Maryllia was doing now.

"It scared the hell out of me," he said, shaking his head. "I couldn't do the cut. My hands were shaking so bad. If Evalycer hadn't been there, it would have been bad."

"The woman has no fear," Samara said. She meant it as a compliment.

"That's what makes her so good at what she does."

"I'll make us dinner while you shower," Samara said.

Jory went into the bathroom and turned on the water. He undressed and stepped into the spray, letting it wash away the grim and the memories of the day. After drying and dressing, he went into the kitchen and found Samara had made them grilled fish and a fresh fruit salad.

After dinner, Jory lay in bed thinking long after Samara had gone to sleep. These Gantians were a big problem.

Chapter Twenty-One

Evalycer parked her rover at the door of her home. On her way home, she changed her mind about the card game and just wanted to go home. She opened the door and felt the heat blast. Having her home closed up for the day had made it like a furnace. Evalycer went through her home, opening windows to let the cool breeze flow through and got a bottle of Pelonsa Reserve from her cabinet. She poured a large glass, slipped off her boots, and sat heavily in a chair. She took a long drink of the alcohol and leaned back in the chair. What a helluva day she'd had. All of them had had. She'd had no idea how it was going to turn out, and Maryllia getting shot with that chemical blast…

She finished the drink, set the glass on the side table, and looked at her hands. Those hands only a few hours ago had been cutting into flesh. Even though she had washed her hands afterwards, Evalycer could still see stains from Maryllia's blood on them. She rubbed her left hand violently with her other hand to get the blood stains off. *There's too much blood shed in this universe. I can't get this off.*

She put her face into those same hands, her elbows resting on her knees. *Maryllia could have died today. How did I manage to save her?* Her emotions welling up inside, she sobbed. It wasn't something that happened very often, but when it did, it was gut-wrenching, ugly sobs. She allowed herself this moment of weakness only once in a while. All of the strain of the past few weeks, and especially that day, came flowing out of her with each sob. Maryllia's wound had been horrendous, and Evalycer, usually sure of herself, hadn't been sure she could take care of it. It had been a relief to hear the doctor say Maryllia would be fine.

Evalycer pulled herself together again, hiccupping the last sob away. She breathed in deeply, wiped her face, and stood up to refill her glass. She went in to shower, scrubbing her hands to get all the blood off of them. After dressing in her night clothes, she finished her drink and climbed into bed, and hoped to sleep well tonight. She was so drained, her body hurt to move.

Evalycer woke up to the sound of traffic going past her home. She realized that in her tired state last night, she'd left all her windows open. Evalycer threw the bed coverings off and padded to the front of the house. She looked outside, then slammed the windows shut.

Not an early riser by nature, it still surprised her that it was well into morning. She thought about going back to bed, but it would take her a long time to get back to sleep now that she was up. *Might as well stay up.*

After breakfast and drinking her Elixir, Evalycer dressed and set out to see Maryllia in the hospital wing of the base. She didn't know what would happen that day, and brought her weapons along. She figured that the Gantians weren't going to just concede quietly. It wasn't her fight, but her loyalty to Maryllia, Tobias, and Jory compelled her to be ready to help. She never thought she'd be part of a team again after leaving the RPF, and yet there she was, part of a team that worked well together and had each other's back.

Getting through the city at that time of day took an hour, but she refused to live within the center of the city near the base. When Evalycer arrived at the base she went directly to the medical bay and the hospital wing to see Maryllia.

When she opened the door, Evalycer saw Jory already there, visiting. "I can come back," Evalycer said, backing out of the room.

"No, come on in," Jory said.

Evalycer came in and shut the door.

"I guess I have you to thank for my surgery," Maryllia said.

"I just cut out the chemical, I didn't really do anything else," Evalycer said.

"Don't be modest," Jory said. "I couldn't do it and you stepped up."

"Well, you're welcome," Evalycer replied. "How are you this morning?"

"Better," Maryllia said. "I can go home later today, but bedrest until tomorrow. The muscle has grown back, but I'll need some physical therapy to get my strength back."

Maryllia's doctor came in. "Okay, my patient needs her rest," he said. "You can come back later to visit."

Jory kissed his sister on the forehead, and Evalycer gave a wave of her hand as they both left the room.

"I didn't want to say anything in there," Jory said. "But Keedu has threatened to hijack more shipments to Foridian."

"Shit," she said, a little too loudly, as two Academy instructors walked by and reprimanded her. "Just mind your own business," she said to them. To Jory, she asked, "Can we fly around Jenubri to put us further away from Startia?"

"We'll have to," he said. "We can't put all of us at risk by flying near Startia."

"I guess you're right," Evalycer said. "We're going to have to do this trip sooner rather than later."

"Since the Gantians hijacked that last shipment, it'll be today."

"When do we leave?"

"In a couple hours."

Evalycer thought for a moment. She'd have to replace Maryllia, and Aiden. She couldn't put Aiden through this again.

"I have to contact some people," she said, turning to leave. "I'm down two crew members."

Jory watched her go. He went to the hangar bay to check on his ship and found Tobias already working on the engines.

"She'll be ready to go soon," Tobias said. "I installed a thruster enhancement to get more energy from the engines, in case we have to outrun any hostiles."

"Excellent," Jory said. "Evalycer is looking for a couple crew members since Maryllia's out and she doesn't trust Aiden to keep his head."

General Frey called them into his office.

"The Elixir will be loaded and ready by the time you're ready to leave," he told them.

"Good," Jory said. "We're flying around Jenubri to avoid dealing with the Gantians."

"I hope that will end this," Frey said. "But I feel they are just starting. I'm adding Tyrian Five as an escort, because you can use all the help you can get now."

"I think Evalycer will agree with you this time," Jory replied.

By the time Evalycer came back, Tobias had finished with their ship. She had found a couple of her pilot friends to replace Maryllia and Aiden.

"Major Vance, Lieutenant Kelly," Evalycer started. "This is Bailey and Jensen."

Jory and Tobias shook hands with the men. "Your Highness," they both said.

"Please, call me Jory," Jory told them.

"Bailey is pretty good at reading minds," Evalycer said. "Not as good as Maryllia, of course, but better than most, and both are excellent pilots."

"You both know what you're getting into, correct?" Jory asked them, half-joking.

"Yes, sir," Bailey said. "We won't crack under pressure."

"Good. Let's get going."

Jory informed Evalycer about the added escort. As he'd guessed, she was happy to have them.

They requested and received permission to take off. The *Silver Reign* started to move out of the hangar bay, Jory and Tobias in Tyrian One, and Fletcher and Yates in Tyrian Five following.

"They will be making another run today," the voice said from the communicator. "You can expect them later today."

"Good," said Keedu. "We'll get them in our tractor beam and take their shipment. You have your supply still?"

"Yes," the voice replied. "I have it hidden away. Only I have access to it. No one else on the planet has been able to drink it since you hijacked the last shipment."

"Very well," Keedu said. "I'll let you know what happens."

Keedu had been angry since the princess's rescue yesterday. He had underestimated her and the crew. The princess was very resourceful and very much in control of her abilities. He had read Sayzan's mind several times since then and hadn't seen anything about Sayzan wanting to take control. It was possible that he now hid the information, now that he'd learned how to do so, but he bet on the princess putting the thoughts in Sayzan's mind in the first place. Keedu hadn't yet learned how to dig deeper into someone's mind to see what they were hiding. *The princess was right*, he thought. *It takes a lot of work and time to learn that ability.*

"The only conclusion I can think of is that she wanted to cause a conflict between us," Keedu had said earlier that day. "So, we make her pay for this."

Now, Keedu and his men were trying to figure out how to do that. His contact on Foridian fed them intel about the shipments, so that would help. They'd have to learn to control their abilities more before they could go after the princess.

***

The *Silver Reign* and its escorts hit light speed and flew straight out from Darantha toward Jenubri. They slowed to sub-light to make the turn past Jenubri, then light speed again past Startia. They hit the asteroid belt further away from Startia and once through, they were beyond Ganta Zay's sensors.

"I hate that we have to stay overnight," Evalycer grumbled into her headset.

"Yeah," Jory replied over the radio. "But that's the regulations."

"I thought I was done with regulations when I left the RPF," she said.

Once past Jenubri, they angled toward Foridian, not making a full turn, to avoid being picked up by the Gantians. They could adjust their heading once they were well past Ganta Zay.

Night had fallen by the time they arrived on Foridian. They landed at the usual spaceport and the Foridian crew unloaded the Elixir crates.

"Sorry the Gantians have forced you to change your plans," Govern Oxmoor told them. "But glad you made it safely this time. How is Lieutenant Vance?"

"She's doing better," Jory said. "If it hadn't been for Evalycer, however, she might not be in as good of shape as she is."

Oxmoor showed them where they would be staying for the night in his residence. They had an entire wing to themselves. He informed the group that dinner would be served shortly and invited them to dine with him and his family.

"Thank you, sir," Jory said. They would all be there.

Jory and his crew thoroughly enjoyed dinner and the company. Governor Oxmoor told them stories of the citizens learning to use their abilities. As they sat at the table, Evalycer had a strange feeling. She couldn't pinpoint it. She didn't see anything and after a quick read of everyone's minds there, she still didn't know what happened.

After dinner, the crew went to their wing of the residence. After Bailey and Jensen went to their rooms, Evalycer stopped Jory and Tobias.

"Something is going on here," she said urgently.

"Why? What happened?" Jory asked.

She told them both about the feeling she'd gotten at dinner and what she'd done. "It was weird," she said.

Jory frowned. This whole Elixir trade with the Foridians had been rife with trouble. Maryllia had felt it, now Evalycer.

"I'll ask Governor Oxmoor tomorrow how the progress is going with their own Elixir facility," Jory said. "Maybe we won't have to do this much longer and then it will be the Foridians' problem."

"I need a card game," Evalycer said. "I need to get rid of some of this stress."

"We'll go with you," Tobias said, looking at Jory.

Jory shrugged. "Sure, why not."

He spoke with the governor, who gave them the use of one of his rovers and told them where they could find what they were looking for.

Jory drove the rover, maneuvering it around the streets of the city. They found the place the governor had suggested. Jory parked the rover off the street and they went inside.

Bright pink and blue lighting lit up the bar area. The tables were more dimly lit, but still well-lit for a card game. They walked up to the bar to get their drinks. Jory didn't want to play cards. He was more or less looking out for Evalycer, who he knew had had a rough couple of days. She hid it well, but she'd let her guard down a couple of times when she thought no one was looking, and in those moments Jory had seen her flexing her hands or pacing outside of her ship. Jory knew she felt the stress more than she let on.

With drink in hand, Evalycer approached a table that didn't look too threatening. Jory and Tobias stood off to the side, watchful of everything around them.

Evalycer downed a few drinks, played a few rounds of the game, won a couple, and was ready to call it a night. The players

179

she played with still hadn't learned how to use their abilities, so she didn't think it was fair to keep playing against them.

They hung out at the bar for a while. Jory didn't drink much, as he wanted to keep an eye on Evalycer. He knew she could take care of herself, but also knew she could be a bit of a hot-head and react without thinking.

"How come you're not drinking?" Evalycer asked him.

"I am," he said, holding up his drink.

"I know that's only your second."

"I'm just not in a drinking mood tonight," he told her. "But you go ahead and have fun."

She winked at Jory, and staggered over to talk to a couple of pilots. He read her mind and they were just swapping stories of trips they'd all done in the past.

Two hours later, Evalycer wanted to leave. She walked out on her own but had a little trouble getting into the rover. Tobias helped her into the back behind Jory. Jory started the rover and they drove toward the governor's residence.

"Holy crap, I needed that," she said.

When they got back to the governor's residence, Evalycer went to her room. She paused at her door. "Thanks for watching out for me tonight," she said.

"No problem," Jory told her. "Good night."

Jory awakened early the next morning. He wanted to get back home as soon as possible, and checked over the ship before breakfast. Tobias joined him a few minutes later.

"Everything look good?" Tobias asked.

"Yeah," Jory said. "I'm just anxious to get out of here. Like Evalycer said, something doesn't feel right."

"I know you worry," Tobias said. "But I agree with you this time. I can't quite put my finger on it."

They went back in to eat breakfast. They saw Evalycer sitting at the table eating with Bailey and Jensen.

"Good morning," Jory said cheerfully.

"Hey," she said. "We leaving soon?"

"Right after we eat," Jory replied. "I'm surprised you're not feeling a little ill this morning."

"I carry toxi-tabs with me."

"I should've known."

They finished breakfast quickly, eager to get back home. Jory and Evalycer thanked the governor for his hospitality, and went to their ships. Fletcher and Yates were already in the hangar, waiting for them.

"Let's get the hell out of here," Evalycer said.

The crew followed Evalycer into the *Silver Reign* as the others went to their respective ships. Once they had clearance, they flew out of the hangar bay, toward home.

"Do you think we need to fly around Jenubri going home?" Tobias asked.

"I don't think so," Jory said hesitantly. "It wouldn't make any sense to hijack the ship now that we've dropped off the load."

"I say we just go for it," Evalycer said in the headset. "Fly the normal route home."

"Copy that," Jory said. They started their route between Startia and Ganta Zay.

When they got nearer Ganta Zay, they started their visual scanning as well as instrument scanning. There looked to be a fighter coming their way.

"Stay on course," Jory told Evalycer. "We'll deal with them."

The *Silver Reign* kept on course with Tyrian Five as their escort. Jory flew his ship to intercept them. He remembered the tractor beam and stayed clear of its range as he engaged the fighter.

The fighter did nothing but fire a few shots over Jory's ship. Tobias returned fire, but the ship wasn't hit. The fighter left as quickly as it came.

"What the hell was that about?" Tobias asked.

"Not sure," Jory said. "But I'd venture to say that they will not let us do the next run easily."

Chapter Twenty-Two

Maryllia left the hospital the next day. She could walk, but needed a cane to take most of her weight. The doctor wanted her to take a leave of absence from her duties, but she wouldn't hear it. The doctor let her do light duty at her desk—no flying.

The following week, Jory, Tobias, and Evalycer checked the invoice as the workers loaded the shipment onto the *Silver Reign*. Jory and Tobias did their usual check of the engines before the trip. Tyrian Five was ready to go as well.

Before they left, they established that going around Jenubri would be their normal route now. It put them far enough away from Startia and well beyond Ganta Zay. As they flew past Startia's sector, however, they saw a line of fighters just sitting there, waiting.

"What the hell is that?" Evalycer asked.

"I don't know," Jory said slowly.

They were about two kilometers away when one of the fighters moved forward. A light on the console came on, indicating the fighter was trying to contact them. Tobias pushed a button so they could listen.

"You will not be able to pass," said a voice in their headsets.

"By whose authority?" Jory asked.

"Keedu of Ganta Zay."

"He has no control over this area," Jory said firmly.

"He has more control than you think," the voice said. "I am Metz. Keedu has hired me to keep you from making your delivery. You will not pass."

Jory did some quick thinking. They were outnumbered and definitely outgunned. Jory and Tobias were good, but not good enough to take on seven fighters at once, even with Tyrian Five and the weapons on the *Silver Reign*.

"I guess Keedu wins this round," Jory said.

"What are you doing?" Evalycer asked sharply. "We have to get this to Foridian, Jory."

"Do you like our odds?" Jory asked incredulously.

Evalycer was silent for a moment. "No," came the sullen reply.

"If we go the regular route, they will hijack the shipment."

The *Silver Reign* started its turn back. Tyrian Five turned to follow. Jory and Tobias sat for a moment longer before they, too, turned back.

When they got near Darantha, Jory called in to land. The general hadn't expected them back so soon and met them in the hangar bay.

"What happened?" he asked.

"We ran into some trouble near Startia's sector," Jory said, giving him the story.

"You're getting soft, Jory," Evalycer said as she raced over to the men. "We could've gotten through there."

"Not with all that fire power they had," Jory said. "We'd have gotten obliterated, or captured. I certainly don't like either scenario."

General Frey held up his hands. Jory and Evalycer stopped ranting. "Major Vance did the right thing. I don't want any of you getting hurt. We'll figure out a way to get the Elixir there."

"And I have an idea, if you want to listen," Jory said to Evalycer.

"What?"

"We use the ship we used to rescue Maryllia to make the runs to Foridian."

"I'm listening," Evalycer said.

"We wouldn't be able to get the whole shipment on board, but we could do several trips throughout the day. It's got that cloaking device, so they shouldn't be able to see us or track us."

"That might work," Frey said.

"It might," Evalycer said thoughtfully.

"Try it tomorrow," the general ordered. "See how much of the shipment you can get on the ship."

"Yes, sir," Jory said.

***

Keedu greeted the squadron when they came back.

"It went well, I presume?" Keedu asked.

"They didn't challenge us at all," Metz said. "They turned and went back home."

"I'm sure they'll try something else in the next couple of days. We'll scan the area and send out patrols to watch for them. We'll get the next Elixir shipment."

Keedu went back to his office and contacted his informer. The shadowed face of a man in a dark hood came into view.

"Your intel was accurate, Garson," Keedu told him. "They were coming around Jenubri and we effectively stopped them as they passed through Startia's sector, well beyond their monitors."

"They may try something else," Garson said. "Some other way to get the shipment to Foridian."

"We'll keep watch for them," Keedu told him. "You'll receive your payment next week."

"I look forward to it," Garson said. "Keep your eyes open, Keedu. They will try again, and next time, we may have to get Startia involved in this."

***

Evalycer awakened early the next morning. She wanted to get her ship to the base as quickly as possible to get this shipment onboard and ready to go. She ate breakfast quickly and downed her Elixir before dressing and heading out the door.

She arrived at the Star Shot Spaceport a few minutes later. Evalycer checked out the engines and especially the cloaking device. Everything seemed to be in as good of shape as she left it from the rescue mission. She started the engine sequence and was soon airborne. It took only a few minutes to fly to the base. She landed the ship near the *Silver Reign*, to make it easier to transfer the shipment from one ship to the other.

Jory and Tobias came in a few minutes later. They were surprised to see Evalycer already working.

"You're here early," Jory said.

"Yeah," Evalycer replied. "I want to get this done as soon as possible. I'm not paid to lollygag around."

Tobias and Jory helped load the Elixir shipment onto the ship. It didn't even hold half of the shipment.

"Three trips," Evalycer said grumpily.

"We should be finished in the same amount of time as doing one trip in the *Silver Reign*," Jory said.

"I hope so. The sooner we can get there and back, the better."

"Are *you* nervous?" Jory asked in disbelief.

"Not in the least," Evalycer said. "It's just a lot of opportunity for the Gantians to hijack any of the shipments."

When they were ready to go, the general gave them last minute instructions.

"If the Gantians try to intercept you, just turn around," he told Jory and Evalycer. "If this doesn't work, the Foridians will have to figure out how to get the shipments there. We're doing it as a favor to them, but I'm not putting anyone else at risk for this."

Jory assured him that he agreed with him, and Evalycer did as well.

They were in the air a few minutes later. Once clear of the planet's gravity, they jumped to light speed. It took them an hour to reach the asteroid belt. They went sub-light through the belt, then cloaked the ship for the rest of the trip to Foridian. Wanting to get this trip done as fast as possible, they hit light speed for only a moment to get to Foridian quickly.

"I thought you were due here yesterday," Governor Oxmoor said as they disembarked.

"We would have been," Jory said. "But we ran into a blockade as we went through Startia's sector. We couldn't get past them, so had to turn back and come up with another plan."

"It seems to have worked out," Oxmoor stated.

"We'll make two more trips here today," Evalycer told him. "Shouldn't be any trouble getting here."

Governor Oxmoor called over his advisor Malin Garrick. "Make sure this shipment gets distributed right away," he said.

"Yes, sir," Garrick said, turning to take care of the shipment.

Once the shipment was unloaded, the crew flew back to Darantha to pick up the second shipment and returned to Foridian with no trouble. Garrick was still seeing to the first shipment, and would continue with the second while Jory and his crew flew back for the last load.

"One more trip," Jory said as they prepared to take off for the third time from Darantha.

"I'll be glad when this trip is done," Maryllia said. "Too many opportunities for something to happen."

"I've been a little wary myself," Evalycer said. "Seems too easy…"

Chapter Twenty-Three

"They will be making one more trip here with the last shipment," Garson said over the communicator. "Their ship is equipped with both a cloaking device and hyper-drive. I don't see how you will be able to stop them this time."

Keedu paced the floor, thinking. A few years ago, he'd gotten his hands on new technology that could detect ships going light speed. Would it work on cloaked ships as well?

"I've got a way to track them," Keedu said finally. "Or at least I hope it will."

He told Garson and Sayzan about the technology. It could read ion trails left by ships going light speed. Combined with the pulse beam that rendered the ship's weapons useless, they'd be able to bring in the ship.

***

The ship dropped out of light speed without warning as they passed Ganta Zay. The cloaking device also failed.

"What the hell happened?" Evalycer exclaimed, frantically looking over the control console. "What happened to my ship?"

Jory looked it over as well. He pushed some buttons, but nothing happened. They were still moving, but just barely. Jory didn't like it at all.

"Can you detect anything?" Jory asked.

Evalycer ran a scan. Nothing came up. Tobias brought up the engine diagnostic, but everything seemed operational.

They tried going back to light speed, but nothing happened.

"We've still got propulsion," Evalycer said. "We gotta get out of here."

She and Jory moved the controller forward and the ship started moving again, albeit much slower than before. Tobias came back a few minutes later. "Nothing is wrong with the engines."

Jory picked up a signal on the scanner. "Fighters coming in fast," he said.

"These Gantians are starting to piss me of," Evalycer stated.

"Can we cloak?" Tobias asked.

Evalycer hit the button. The readout indicated they had cloaked. They wouldn't know for sure until the Gantian fighters came up and indicated they could be seen.

"We have to get some distance between us and them," Jory said.

Evalycer tried to get a little more speed out of her ship. She dropped life support to fifty percent, but didn't dare decloak. It gave the engines about twenty percent more power. They started to move out of range of the Gantian fighters. The fighters didn't give any indication they saw the ship.

***

"I know we got them," said Sayzan. "They decloaked briefly, but then cloaked again."

"Follow their last known trajectory," Keedu said. "They can't be moving very fast now."

Sayzan looked at the screen and plotted where they could be headed and gave the coordinates to the fighters. They reported back that they couldn't find them.

"Their ship has to be leaving some sort of ionic trail," Keedu said.

The pilots in the fighters scanned the area for ionic trails. It was hard to pinpoint with all the other traffic going through the area. They thought they found something and started to follow.

189

***

"We've got company," Tobias said.

Jory looked at his screen. "Gantians," he said.

"How can they be following us if they can't see us?" Evalycer asked.

"Ionic trail," Tobias said. "Every ship leaves some kind of trail that is detectable. All they'd have to do is know where we were headed."

"Which they do," Jory said.

"Well that's fucking great," Evalycer said. She thought a moment. "Can we throw them off by taking a detour?"

"What do you mean?" Jory asked.

"Drop into the traffic pattern between Monta Nesta and Foridian. We'll stay far enough away to avoid any scanners from them, and Ganta Zay won't be able to find us with all the other ships there. We'll head toward Monta Nesta, then once we've gone a few kilometers, we turn back toward Foridian. They won't know where to look for us."

"It could work," Jory said slowly. "Let's do it."

Evalycer and Jory turned the controller into the traffic pattern toward Monta Nesta. They remained cloaked to not draw attention to themselves. Once they felt it had been sufficient time and distance, they turned back toward Foridian.

"Do you see anything?" Evalycer asked Tobias.

"Nope," Tobias replied. "I think that did it."

"Keep monitoring," Jory suggested. "They are resourceful and determined. We need to be alert until we get to Foridian."

Tobias kept actively monitoring while Evalycer and Jory piloted the ship. They arrived on Foridian half an hour later. Jory contacted Governor Oxmoor to let him know they would need to repair their ship before heading back home.

190

"What happened?" Oxmoor asked once they landed.

"Somehow the Gantians were able to find us," Jory said. "I don't know how, but they made us drop to sub-light speed and decloak. We were able to cloak again, but our hyper-drive is shot."

"Can you fix it here?" Oxmoor asked.

"I'm sure we can," Tobias said, looking at Evalycer. "Between the three of us, we'll get it going again."

"Let me know if you need anything," the governor said. "I feel responsible for these things happening to you."

"It's not your fault the Gantians keep attacking us," Jory said.

While the shipment was being unloaded, the three of them started working on the engines. Tobias knew most engines inside and out, so with Evalycer's direction, he ran diagnostics on the engines to see what happened.

"And what the hell was this…thing…they used to make us drop into sub-light speed?" Jory wanted to know.

"That's the million-credit question, isn't it?" Evalycer said. "It better not have hurt my ship or there will be hell to pay—by the Gantians."

Jory contacted General Frey at the base, to let him know what took place. "If you can find anything that will help us figure out what's wrong with the engines and what the Gantians used to do this, it would be helpful," Jory said.

"I'll get our best men on it," Frey said. "Keep us posted on your timeline on getting back."

Tobias looked over all the information on his read-out. The hyper-drive was fried. Whatever the Gantians had used to stop the ship had been directed at the hyper-drive to render it inoperable.

"Can you fix it?" Evalycer asked.

"Maybe," Tobias said. "But the circuitry will need to be replaced. It will take some time."

"So we're stuck here overnight again?"

"Looks like it."

"Damn it," Evalycer said, and she stomped into the ship to sulk.

"What's her problem now?" Tobias asked.

"She hates being stuck anywhere," Jory said. "She just wants to get this job done for the week."

Evalycer came out of the ship half an hour later to help Tobias with the engine circuitry. Governor Oxmoor supplied the items needed to repair the ship from his own spaceport. Tobias gathered the items together and started working on it. While he worked on the circuit board, Evalycer worked on taking the engine apart and replacing what had been damaged in there.

"How bad is it?" Jory asked, watching her work.

"Not as bad I as had initially thought," she said. "But bad enough to where we have to replace a lot of stuff."

It took Tobias an hour to get the circuitry back together and working. Evalycer managed to get the engines up and running after a couple of hours. It was too late to test the engines, so they decided to go to bed early to get an early start the next day. The governor graciously invited them to stay at his residence for the night.

Early the next morning, the three of them took a test flight around Foridian to check the engines. They tested the hyper-drive and the ship was able to go light speed again. Jory thanked Governor Oxmoor for his hospitality and they started their flight back home to Darantha.

Chapter Twenty-Four

"You're going to have to do better when they do their next run to Foridian," Garson told Keedu.

"They are certainly creative when it comes to escaping," Keedu said.

"I'm going to take charge of their capture next week," Garson said.

Keedu wasn't happy with that information. Even though Garson had no intention of taking over the planet, Keedu still felt betrayed. This was *his* planet, *his* operation, and he wasn't going to be told he wasn't good enough.

"There is no need for that," Keedu told him. "I have things under control."

"That's why they got away? Because you have everything 'under control'? I know what they are capable of, I'll be there to make sure we can anticipate what they will do next."

"Yes, sir," Keedu said tersely. He punched the button to disengage the communicator.

He'd have to come up with a plan to get the Elixir shipment and show Garson he was capable of doing it.

The following week, Keedu and Sayzan were ready for Darantha's Elixir ship to come by. They had their plan ready to execute. Garson had arrived earlier that day to see that the plan went smoothly. Keedu hadn't seen the man before. His clothes were dark, and only his mouth showed, the rest of his face covered in shadow. His short stature didn't indicate a very strong person, but Keedu knew he had strength and mind-reading abilities from the Elixir.

"Hello," Keedu said as he met the man in the hangar bay. He wasn't happy to see him, so didn't pretend to be. He didn't extend his hand, and neither did Garson.

"I am Garson," he said. "The ship should be going by here in about an hour. Are you sure your plan is ready?"

"I am sure," Keedu said, not attempting to hide his displeasure in having his plans questioned. He knew he couldn't hide his feelings from Garson anyway.

"Good," Garson said. "Once you have your shipment, I will expect a shipment of the mineral to be shipped to my planet."

"It will be done, as it always has been," Keedu said. "You'd be wise to not question my intentions. I have never given you any reason to doubt this arrangement."

"No," Garson said. "But I hear you are getting more aggressive and therefore may not be thinking straight."

"Everything is fine," Keedu snapped.

Garson said no more about it. They watched the monitor, waiting for the Elixir ship to appear.

Sayzan noticed a new blip appear on the monitor. "Get the beam ready!" Sayzan shouted.

Garson watched as a whirl of activity started. Sayzan manned the disruptor beam, another technician the tractor beam, and Keedu gave the order to send out fighters to drive the ship into the tractor beam.

"The ship has disappeared," Sayzan said. He threw the switch to send out the beam that disrupts the hyper-drive and, temporarily, the cloaking device. It worked. The ship appeared on the monitor again.

"The ships should be in range in three minutes," Keedu told Garson.

***

"Damn it!" Evalycer said. "They did it again."

"Hit the cloaking button again," Jory said quickly.

Tobias did so, and the ship cloaked, but only for a moment.

"Shit!" Evalycer exclaimed. "We can't cloak and we've only got sub-light engines."

"I'll go see if I can figure something out," Tobias said, and he ran down to the engine compartment.

"I'll charge the weapon," Jory said, and he ran down the corridor to the weapon station. He threw switches on the control panel near the weapons, and the lights indicated they were charging. He turned on a monitor near one weapon, to see how close the Gantians were getting. They were nearly in range.

"I can't outrun them, Jory," Evalycer said. "You'll have to shoot them."

The fighters got closer and once in range, Jory started firing on them. But nothing happened. Everything showed that the weapons were charged, but they wouldn't fire.

"Son of a bitch," Jory said. "They killed the weapons, too."

"How's the engines coming, Tobias?" Evalycer asked.

"Not good," he replied. "I'm pretty much hot-wiring it. I'll let you know when to try it."

The fighters came and started to nudge the ship toward Ganta Zay. Evalycer tried to correct course, but every time she did, the fighters fired over the ship, driving them nearer the planet until Evalycer felt the pull of the tractor beam.

Jory grabbed three cans of Elixir out of the shipment for them to drink, in case they ended up having an extended stay on the planet again. He tossed a can to Tobias in the engine compartment and handed a can to Evalycer, who looked ready to fight anything in her way.

"Don't upset them," he told her.

"Don't upset *them*?" she said incredulously. "They broke my ship and you don't want me to upset them? Fuck that."

"That's not what I mean. Don't antagonize them. They are already more aggressive because of the Elixir. We don't want to provoke them into doing anything."

Evalycer considered what he said, and nodded. "I'll do my best," she said.

Tobias continued to work on the engines until they were in the hangar bay of Keedu's building.

"Not sure if they'll work," Tobias said, coming up to the cockpit again. "No way to tell."

Once the ship landed in the hangar bay, Keedu ordered them to come out. Jory stepped out first, followed by Tobias, then Evalycer.

"Oh, look," Keedu said. "My favorite hostage is back." The men laughed.

"Pleasure's all yours, Keedu," Evalycer said.

"Welcome back, gentlemen," Keedu said, addressing Jory and Tobias. "So glad you could stop in again."

"What do you want from us now?" Jory asked.

"All I want is the Elixir shipment. Oh, and someone to teach us more about it. You three will do nicely."

Jory noticed another man standing off to the side. "Who is this?" he asked.

"This is my silent partner," Keedu said. "You don't need to concern yourself with him for now."

Keedu motioned for his men to start unloading the Elixir from the ship. "We're short, but it will do for now," said Keedu. "I know you've been trying so hard to get the Elixir to Foridian without us knowing, but—we know."

Sayzan put restraints on the three of them and took them to the same room Evalycer, Aiden, and Maryllia had shared when they were taken captive before.

"Home sweet home," Evalycer said. Sayzan took of the restraints and shoved them further into the room and locked the door. "So, what now?" she asked, looking to Jory.

"We'll have to wait and see what they have in store for us," Jory said. "In the meantime, we have to figure out how to escape."

"It's impossible," Evalycer told him. "We know we can unlock the door, but they will have guards out there."

"We can figure something out. All of us have strong abilities. We just need a plan."

"I tried reading the 'silent partner's' mind," Evalycer said. "But I couldn't see anything. It was blank."

"I don't like the guy," Tobias said. "I get a bad feeling from him, like he's up to something and I should know him, but I don't know how or where I know him."

"He's definitely learned to use his abilities to their fullest extent," Jory remarked. "I wonder how he fits into all this."

They tried to formulate a plan, but without knowing what they were up against, it was difficult. They didn't have to wait for long, however, to see what Keedu had in mind. Sayzan came to their room half an hour later.

"Keedu wants to see the woman," he said.

Evalycer started to move, but Jory held out his hand to stop her. "She's not going alone," he said. "One of us needs to go, too."

"Why?" Sayzan asked angrily. "Keedu only wants her."

"Because even though she can handle herself," Jory said over Evalycer's protests. "I want to make sure everyone stays safe. One of us is going with her."

Sayzan contacted Keedu on his communicator and told him what was going on. He put the communicator away and said, "He can come with us," Sayzan said, pointing to Tobias. "You are to stay. Your abilities are strong, and Keedu doesn't want to deal with you right now."

"Fine," Jory said. He nodded to Tobias, who followed Evalycer to the door where Sayzan put restraints on the both of them.

Sayzan took Evalycer and Tobias to Keedu's office. The silent partner was also there, sitting to the side, watching. Sayzan took the restraints off of them.

"So," Keedu began. "Prince Jordan doesn't trust me to be a gentleman so he sent a bodyguard. His reputation with his abilities demands that he stays in his room. Now, Miss Nichols, you are going to help us learn to control our abilities better."

"The hell I am," Evalycer stated. "For one, I'm not a teacher. For two, I'm not going to help you even if I knew how."

Evalycer suddenly dropped to her knees, clutching her stomach. "You'll help us, or I can make it hurt more," Keedu said.

Using his telekinetic ability, Tobias picked up a cup from Keedu's desk and sent it straight into his head. It broke his concentration, and Evalycer stopped writhing. Keedu put his hand up to his head where the cup had struck him, and saw blood. His eyes narrowed as his face contorted into a scowl. He walked over and backhanded Tobias across the face, knocking him down. His strength ability was evident.

"Don't you *ever* do that again," he seethed. "I see Prince Jordan isn't the only one we have to watch out for."

Tobias spit blood from his cut lip. Evalycer helped him to his feet.

"You both will help me," Keedu said coldly. "Or I'm going to start hurting people, and I don't mean just you. I'm not happy with how the princess pitted us against each other when she was teaching us. I will go after her as well. You both think about that until I have you brought back here." He nodded at Sayzan, who put the restraints back on them and took them back to their room.

"What happened?" Jory asked when he saw Tobias's face.

"He underestimated our abilities," Tobias said. "He attacked Evalycer, so I hit him in the head with a cup and drew some blood."

"It looks like it's not me you have to worry about pissing him off," Evalycer said sarcastically. She got an ice pack from the freezer for Tobias's lip. "He still wants us to teach them how to control their abilities," she said. "He says he's going to start hurting people if we don't comply. He doesn't mean us, Jory. He means your sister. He's angry because she made them attack each other when she was teaching them."

"Which means he'll have to somehow launch an attack on Darantha," Jory said, thinking. "We need to be as vague as we can be when we teach them how to control their abilities. Buy us some time."

"And who is this other guy?" Evalycer asked. "I don't like him."

"Whoever he is, he's got Keedu concerned," Tobias said.

Keedu made them wait for a couple hours before he sent for Evalycer and Tobias. "You're not coming," Sayzan told Jory as he put the restraints on the other two.

Sayzan didn't take them to Keedu's office this time. He took them to a conference room where Keedu and several other men, including the silent partner, waited.

"You're going to teach us how to control our telekinetic abilities," Keedu told them.

"How do you even know you have the ability?" Evalycer asked.

Keedu concentrated on a tablet on the table. He made it slide a few centimeters to the left. "That's how I know," he said.

Evalycer sighed, looking to Tobias. He nodded his head slightly to Evalycer, to get her to continue as planned.

"You have the basics," she said. "You have to think and concentrate on the object, almost willing it to do what you want it to do."

She looked around and saw Sayzan concentrating on a stylus for the tablet. His face grew red as he concentrated. It wouldn't budge.

"Why isn't it working?" Sayzan demanded.

"I don't know," Evalycer said. "Maybe you're not concentrating hard enough."

"I am concentrating on the object!" he shouted.

"Try again," Tobias said.

Sayzan tried again. He made the object twitch, but nothing else.

"You have to tell it what to do," the man said from the corner. "You can't just think 'Move'. You have to give it direction."

Tobias glared at the man. Sayzan tried again, and this time he successfully moved it a short distance on the table.

They spent another fifteen minutes working on making objects move. Keedu wanted to work on other abilities.

"Tell me about seeing into the future," he asked.

Evalycer knew that this was one ability that would be hard to master, even if they did tell them exactly how to do it. It had taken her weeks to learn to do it consistently. But she wasn't going to help them out by telling them how to do it correctly.

"Concentrate on a period of time you want to see," Evalycer started. "You have to focus on that time frame."

She and Tobias watched as the men tried to focus on seeing the future. Keedu closed his eyes, but after a few moments, his eyes flew open. "I'm not seeing anything."

"What she said is true," the man said. "But you have to relax, clear your mind, then focus on seeing the future." He rounded on Evalycer. "Why are you deliberately trying to thwart their progress?" he asked.

"I told you I'm not a teacher," Evalycer told him. "Why don't you teach them since you seem to have it all figured out?"

"You'd better start teaching us properly," Keedu said, his voice rising. "Or I will make sure that the faction on Startia knows where to find you."

Evalycer's heart seemed to stop beating for a moment. How did they know about that?

"You're bluffing," Evalycer said flatly.

"What are they talking about?" Tobias asked, looking at Evalycer sharply.

"Did I let out a secret?" Keedu asked with mock concern. "Your team doesn't know about this little bit of info, do they?"

"They know enough," Evalycer said.

"It seems that before she was a member of the Royal Planet Fleet, Evalycer Nicholls was a member of a faction on Startia that set out to take care of Governor Atouu's regime," Keedu said.

"Yeah, well, you would, too, if you knew how he operated," Evalycer said, trying to sound unconcerned, but her stomach was reeling.

"If she were to ever go back to Startia, or even if they knew she was near, they would capture her and torture her before killing her. She really pissed them off," Keedu said.

"And all I have to do is contact one person there and she'd be history. So," the man said. "You'd better start doing things properly."

"Who is this that you keep listening to?" Tobias asked, and the man's hood flew off, revealing pale hair and skin. Malin Garrick, Governor Oxmoor's advisor, sat in the chair.

"What the hell?" Evalycer asked, shocked. "This is incredible."

Garrick stood up and angrily strode over to Tobias. "You're going to wish you hadn't done that," he said.

Garrick grabbed Tobias and held a knife to his throat. Evalycer, using her telekinetic ability, made the knife fly a few meters and drop to the floor. Garrick let go of Tobias. Keedu punched Tobias in the jaw, knocking him to the floor as Garrick focused his attention on Evalycer, pulling her into a head lock. Tobias stood up and when he saw Garrick with Evalycer, he stopped. It was the first time he'd seen fear in Evalycer's eyes.

"I should turn you over to the faction right now!" Garrick growled.

Evalycer used her ability to bring pain to Garrick's right side. He released her, but punched her in the face.

"Take them back to their room," Garrick said. "Until I decide what to do with them."

Sayzan and two other men grabbed Tobias and Evalycer roughly and led them back to their room.

"What the hell is going on out there?" Jory asked when he saw that Tobias had been hurt again and Evalycer had a bruise forming on her left cheek.

"The silent partner is Malin Garrick," Evalycer told him quickly. "He's the one behind all these hijackings."

"What?" Jory asked in disbelief.

"It's true," Tobias confirmed. "Garrick is the one telling the Gantians what to do and how to do it."

"We gotta get out of here, Jory," Evalycer said. "He'll kill us next time, I have no doubt. He also knows about Startia."

"What is this about Startia that he's got over you?" Tobias asked.

Jory looked at Evalycer, who nodded. Jory told Tobias the whole story.

Tobias sat in silence after hearing the account of the events.

"I'm sorry we didn't tell you about this," Evalycer said. "It's not something that I'm proud of, and I've tried to forget about it. I never in a million years thought it would ever come up again."

Tobias cleared his throat. "I'm sorry that happened to you," he started. "Is there anything else we need to know about?"

Evalycer shook her head. "That's all the sordid details of my past."

With the story out in the open, they quickly devised a plan to get out that they hoped would work. They knew there were guards stationed outside of their door. They could easily unlock the door with their abilities. All three of them were capable of using whatever means to hurt the Gantians. They would have to use more force to kill them or at least render them unconscious in order to escape. All three of them had been trained by the RPF, so none of them had any qualms about killing someone, if necessary.

They were concerned with how much the guards had learned about using their abilities. Evalycer had tried to be unclear when telling them how to use them. Garrick had stepped in to tell them how to do it. He'd learned, of course, from Samara, who was the best instructor on learning to use one's abilities. It worked to their advantage that the guards most likely hadn't been able to practice how to use them. They'd have to go on that assumption for now.

Now, they looked around the room for anything they could use as a weapon. There were utensils for eating, but they wouldn't do much damage. Jory grabbed a glass from the counter. He grabbed a towel from the kitchen and wrapped it around the glass, then set it on the floor and stomped on it. The glass broke into a couple of pieces they could use. Jory gave one each to Tobias and Evalycer. "What about you?" Evalycer asked.

Jory looked around again. The cabinets in the kitchen area had decorative metal pieces. Using his strength ability, he pulled one off and shaped it into a point.

"Okay, we have our weapons," Tobias said. "How do we get out?"

"We'll have to be fast," Jory said. "We'll have to try and go out the same way we did last time—through the hangar bay. We just have to keep moving downward. We'll have to power up the ship quickly and take off before they can get that damn tractor beam on us."

They took a few minutes to clear their heads and relax. They needed to focus on what they needed to do without any distractions, and not have to think at all about what they were doing, relying on instinct as much as possible.

"Are you ready?" Jory asked Tobias and Evalycer.

"Ready," Evalycer replied.

"Let's do this," Tobias said.

Jory took a deep breath and blew it out quickly. He unlocked the door. The guard standing next to the door checked the handle and found it unlocked. He opened the door and Jory was ready for him. He stabbed the guard in the throat with his weapon. As he stepped out into the corridor, the three other guards pointed their weapons at them. Jory, Tobias, and Evalycer used their telekinetic ability to knock the guards down or push their weapons aside as they ran toward them. Using her Strength ability, Evalycer swung her arm with the glass piece in hand, hitting a guard in the face, then spun around and stabbed the guard again in the left side. The guard fell to the ground, in pain and bleeding profusely. Tobias shoved his glass shard into a guard's neck, then sliced the guard's throat under his jaw. Jory kicked one of the guards in the stomach, knocking him down again. He jumped onto him as he lay on the floor and stuck his metal piece into the guard's chest, killing him.

Tobias wiped the sweat off his face as Jory looked around. "We gotta move," Jory said quietly. Panting heavily, they ran down the corridor to the stairwell. Jory opened the door a crack to look down the stairs. "Looks clear," he said. He used his ability to see ahead to confirm, then nodded, and they started their descent down the stairs.

The stairway ended, they knew, at the control room. They would have to figure out a way to get across the room to the door that took them down to the hangar bay.

"We don't have the luxury of an alarm taking everyone away from the control room like last time," Evalycer remarked.

Jory thought a moment. "Who says we don't?" he asked, and soon an alarm sounded. Everyone started to clear the area. Evalycer looked at him inquiringly. "Fire alarm," he told her. They watched as everyone filed out. The also heard people coming down the stairs behind them.

"Mix in with the others," Jory whispered. They opened the door and walked out like they needed to clear everyone out, fanning out to check that everyone got out. They made it to the other door as people started coming out of the stairwell door they had just come from. The lock Jory had destroyed last time had been replaced.

Tobias closed the door quickly behind them. "Brilliant," he said.

They went down the last level to the hangar bay. They saw their ship with only two guards on it. There were a few people in the hangar bay, as people started to file in and head out because of the alarm.

The three of them moved along the walls, staying in the shadows and behind the boxes and bins throughout the bay. A group of people went by their ship. Jory, Tobias, and Evalycer ran and fell in behind them. As they passed the ship, they noticed the opened hatch. Evalycer pulled down the ladder and they quickly climbed inside and closed the hatch.

"We have to get this thing airborne," Evalycer said, setting her weapon on the console. She started flipping switches to start the engine sequence, but would wait to start them until everything was up and running. They didn't want to draw attention to themselves.

When the console indicated the engines were ready, Evalycer hit the button to start the engines, firing them up. The guards outside the ship turned and saw the hatch was shut. They fired on the ship, but their lasers didn't have much impact.

"We have to make it past the tractor beam before they engage it," Jory said. Evalycer maneuvered the ship toward the hangar doors, which were closing. She moved the controller forward quickly and turned the ship sideways to clear the doors before they shut.

***

"Shut the doors, now!" Keedu bellowed. The technician pushed the button to shut the doors. Keedu watched as the ship turned on its side and made it out before the doors closed. "That tractor beam better be ready," he said. The men scrambled to make sure the tractor beam *was* ready.

***

"If the hyper-drive is fixed, we're going to do something a little dangerous," Evalycer said. "Hang on."

"What's that?" Jory asked.

Evalycer hit the button for light speed before they had cleared Ganta Zay's gravity. The ship shook and rattled, but the engines engaged. An alarm sounded, indicating gravity. Evalycer flipped a switch and killed the alarm to override the fail-safe. The ship jumped to light speed. Fifteen seconds later, the ship came back to sub-light speed, just before entering the asteroid belt.

"Looks like your hot-wiring job worked," Jory said to Tobias.

"I learned that trick a few years ago," Evalycer told Jory and Tobias. "Saved my neck more than once."

"That was incredibly dangerous," Jory said. "How did you know we wouldn't hit the asteroids?"

"I know my ship, and I know my way around the galaxy," she replied. "The fail-safe detects gravity, no matter where it is, in front or behind. I knew the location of the asteroid belt, and turned off the fail-safe so we could make the jump to escape the tractor beam."

Evalycer followed the security through the asteroid belt, then, with the fail-safe fully engaged again, she put the ship into light speed for the trip home.

Chapter Twenty-Five

Jory, Tobias, and Evalycer arrived back on Darantha safely an hour later. They landed in the hangar bay, and went in to see General Frey to tell him what happened.

"Malin Garrick, the Governor's advisor, is behind the attacks," Jory told him.

"What?" Frey said in disbelief. "Why would he be behind this?"

"We don't know," Evalycer said. "He didn't tell us anything."

"We'll need to contact Governor Oxmoor right away," the general said. General Frey himself contacted Governor Oxmoor.

"General Frey," Governor Oxmoor greeted on the communicator.

"Governor Oxmoor," Frey said. "My crew has just returned home from another hostage situation on Ganta Zay."

"Those people really need to be taken care of," the governor said.

"Yes, they do, and we'll need your help to do so."

"What do you mean?"

"Your advisor, Malin Garrick, is the one behind the attacks."

"What?" Oxmoor said, his eyes widened in stunned anger. "Garrick had been acting strange lately, but we thought it was because he wasn't used to the Elixir. He's been getting more aggressive with each day."

"Has anyone else shown any of these signs or behaviors?" General Frey asked.

"Not that's been reported. Why?"

The general turned to Jory. "It seems that the Gantians are the only race that turns aggressive when they drink the Elixir," Jory said.

"Are you suggesting that Garrick is a Gantian?" Oxmoor asked.

"Yes," Frey said. "We'll need your help in capturing him."

"Whatever you need, it's yours," Oxmoor replied.

Jory looked at General Frey, who nodded. "My crew will be there in two hours," Jory said. "Do you know where he is?"

"He's not here at the moment," Oxmoor said. "He's been gone for a few days."

"He's been on Ganta Zay all this time. We'll find him if he's not there when we arrive. Frey out." He turned to Jory. "Get a crew together and go to Foridian to capture Garrick. Take Lieutenant Nicholls's ship. I'll have a couple of squadrons on stand-by, for when you need it."

"Yes, sir," Jory said. He looked at Evalycer. "Get your ship ready to go. Take Tobi with you to check on the engines."

"We've got to do more than just rig the hyper-drive before we can go," Evalycer said.

"We'll make that our first priority," Frey said. "I'll send our best engine experts to help with the engines," he told Tobias.

"Thank you, sir," Tobias said. He and Evalycer ran to the ship to start the repairs to the hyper-drive. On his way to the ship, Jory contacted Samara.

"This is just a quick call," he told her. "We're heading back to Foridian. We've had a break in this Gantian problem and we're heading to Foridian."

"Be careful," Samara said. "I'm tired of half my family getting taken hostage."

"We will. I love you."

"I love you, too."

Jory reached the ship as Evalycer and Tobias were taking the engine circuitry apart to repair and replace the circuits. A couple of officers from Engineering came over with supplies and schematics to help them get the engines up and running again.

Half an hour later, Evalycer and Tobias took the ship out to test the drive.

"How'd it go?" Jory asked when they returned.

"Everything is ready to go," Evalycer told him, gathering up the tools. "The weapons are working now, too."

She checked the weapons on her belt, making sure she had her knife with her. Jory and Tobias both had their blaster with them, as well as their own knives. They got on board and started the flight sequence to take off. They were given priority clearance to leave the hangar bay.

Once clear of the planet, they jumped to light speed. They came back to sub-light when they had to make the turn around Jenubri, and again when they got to the asteroid field. After passing through the field, Evalycer cloaked the ship for extra protection, then hit the hyper-drive again.

They arrived on Foridian fifteen minutes later. They uncloaked as they approached and requested permission to land in the governor's spaceport. Governor Oxmoor met them as they got off the ship.

"Garrick has not returned yet," he told them.

"That doesn't surprise me," Jory said. "He's probably still seething over our escape from the Gantians."

"I don't understand how he can be involved with those criminals. We had him thoroughly vetted before hiring him."

"We'll wait for him, but not for long." Jory's meaning was clear: if he didn't show up on Foridian, they'd look for him on Ganta Zay.

***

Garrick was furious. He couldn't believe that they'd gotten away and evaded the tractor beam. Keedu silently watched Garrick pace around the room.

"They know who I am now," Garrick said. "I can't go back to Foridian."

"How do you know they've told Oxmoor about you?" Keedu asked hesitantly.

"Of course they've told him!" Garrick shouted. "It was the first thing they did once they arrived back home. They're not idiots."

"What's your plan now?"

Garrick paced the floor, thinking. He knew that the RPF would be hunting for him. He knew he couldn't go back to Foridian now. The RPF would be there soon, if they weren't there already, and Governor Oxmoor would also be looking for him.

This wasn't what he'd had planned from the beginning. He'd wanted to just live quietly on Foridian, being the governor's advisor. Garrick knew politics well, and was well-studied in other races, so when he'd applied for the position of advisor, he'd been at the top of the list. Once they'd done the background check and passed, they'd hired him. He had hidden the fact that he was a Gantian. He knew there was no future for him on Ganta Zay, with the pirates running the planet.

Back then, Keedu wasn't the administrator, but was being groomed for the position by Arnik. Keedu was a quick study, and when Arnik passed away, he stepped seamlessly into the role. He had his own advisor, Sayzan, so Garrick left for Foridian.

No one had known that the Elixir would affect Gantians the way it did. The Elixir made Gantians more aggressive and have double the strength ability of others. Governor Oxmoor had questioned Garrick about his strength ability, but Garrick had passed it off as normal, but when Garrick started showing the aggressive behavior he'd thus far kept hidden from the governor, Oxmoor had told him to take some time off, attributing it to stress.

Garrick had decided to go back to Ganta Zay. With his new-found strength, Garrick had easily persuaded Keedu to hijack the shipments to Foridian, thinking that he would work his way into Keedu's position. Keedu seemed to fear him and his abilities, of which mind reading and telekinesis had emerged as well.

"We're going to make sure that we keep getting the Elixir here," Garrick said. "If Darantha won't negotiate with us, we'll have to take it from them." He turned to Keedu. "We're launching the attack today."

***

Jory and his team waited for over an hour for Garrick to come back before deciding to go after him. Jory contacted General Frey.

"We're going to need back-up," he told the general. "Garrick hasn't returned, so we're going to have to go get him, which means he may not come peacefully."

"I'll send two squadrons there," Frey said.

"Make sure they fly around Startia," Jory reminded. "Otherwise Keedu will see them coming."

General Frey assured Jory that the squadrons would do just that. "They'll be there in little more than an hour."

"Copy that," Jory said, and the general's picture faded from view.

In the time it took the squadrons to get to Foridian, Jory, Tobias, and Evalycer devised a plan to get Garrick and Keedu. They both were to blame for this mess. Jory received a message, saying the squadrons were five minutes away. Governor Oxmoor had made arrangements for the squadrons to land near his residence, so Jory could easily coordinate with them.

"His actions tell us he's Gantian," Jory told the squadrons. "We need to capture him and Keedu if we can, but I also say kill them if we must. This is personal. If anyone has a problem with that, you may as well leave now."

No one moved. They all knew and respected Maryllia, and wanted the Gantians to pay for taking her hostage and hurting her in the process. It was also personal to Jory because they had taken Tobias and Evalycer.

Jory, Tobias, and Evalycer went over everything they had learned about the Gantians since this conflict had started. They also made sure everyone had a mask to wear if they ever had to leave their ship. Governor Oxmoor had his squadrons ready to go as well. This was his fight, too. His orders for his squadron were the same as Jory's: capture if possible, kill if needed.

When everything was clear, Jory told Governor Oxmoor that they were ready to go to Ganta Zay to take care of Keedu and Garrick.

"Good luck," Oxmoor told them.

They ran to their ships. Evalycer's ship wasn't the fastest, but it had enough fire power to hold its own with the squadron fighters. She had Tobias charge the weapons right away.

Once in the air, Jory checked to make sure all fighters could hear him.

"We hear you loud and clear," Tyrian Five told him. The Foridian fighters acknowledged as well.

"Stay alert and be ready," Jory told them. "They'll know we're coming very soon."

Chapter Twenty-Six

"We've got company," Sayzan said, looking up from the computer read-out.

Keedu and Garrick looked at the screen. "Why are Foridian fighters coming here?" Keedu asked.

"It's not just Foridian fighters," Garrick snapped. "It's Prince Jordan and his squadron, too."

Keedu turned to Sayzan. "Send out four squadrons to intercept!" he ordered.

"Yes, sir," Sayzan said, and he pushed a button to sound the alarm. The men ran to their ships and once airborne, Keedu gave them instructions.

"They're coming to take us out," Keedu told them. "They will take away our way of life now with the Elixir. They will come after me and Garrick. Make sure that doesn't happen."

The ships acknowledged. They flew out to engage the RPF ships before they came to Ganta Zay.

"It's time to set our plan in motion," Garrick said. Keedu nodded and sent the signal for the rest of the squadrons to head to Darantha.

***

"Gantian fighters coming our way," Tobias said.

"This is Tyrian One," Jory said into the headset. "We have Gantian ships headed our way. Your lasers will not have much effect on their ships because of the duratatium. You have to aim for the cockpit, where there is no metal."

"Copy that," came the replies.

The Gantian ships came in fast. Tobias went to the laser cannon and fired on the ships as they came in.

"This ship is huge compared to the fighters," Jory said, banking hard to the left to avoid a collision. He barely cleared the ship.

"Yeah, it wasn't made for battle," Evalycer said. "The cannon is there to defend ourselves, not engage in combat."

The squadrons held their own with the Gantians. They had to pinpoint their shots to aim for the cockpits to disable or kill and they destroyed many of the Gantian ships. The skill level of the RPF, along with their abilities and smaller ships helped them thin out the Gantians.

"What's this?" Tobias asked.

"What's wrong?" Jory replied.

"I've got new signals leaving Ganta Zay from the far side of the planet."

Jory looked at the screen. About twenty ships were leaving the planet, fast.

"They're leaving in a hurry," Jory remarked. "Tyrian Five," Jory said into the headset. "We've got a new group of signals leaving Ganta Zay. We need to follow them, and we need you to come with us."

"Copy that," Tyrian Five replied.

The two ships broke off from the fighting to follow the ships. Jory feared where they might be headed. The ships flew straight through the asteroid field without the security escort. Evalycer followed, flying around and under the asteroids, nearly colliding with a few. The smaller Gantian ships maneuvered easily through the field without having to slow much. Evalycer and Jory had to cut back on speed to get through. When they emerged from the field, they couldn't visually see them, but just caught sight of them on the screen—heading for Darantha.

"Tyrian squadron, this is Tyrian One," Jory said.

"Copy, Tyrian One," came the reply.

"Gantian ships are headed to Darantha," he said. "Break off from the fighting and head home."

"We're on our way," said Tyrian Eight, and the squadrons left the fighting to head back home.

"Governor Oxmoor," Jory started.

"We see what's happening, Major Vance," said the governor. "We'll take care of what's left of the fighters here. Be careful."

***

"Are they gone?" Garrick asked.

Keedu looked at the screen. "Yes," he said. "All of Darantha's fighters took off after our fighters. The Foridians have only a few fighters out there."

"Call in our ships," Garrick said. "Once the Foridians have left the area, we can head out."

Keedu called the rest of the ships still fighting back to the base. Two Foridian fighters followed, but only for a short distance, then they, too, turned back home.

Garrick, Keedu, and Sayzan went to the hangar bay. Keedu and Sayzan checked over the ship, making sure their weapons were functional and the cloaking device had been installed properly. Once everything was in order, Garrick joined them onboard.

"Darantha is about to get one hell of a surprise," Garrick said.

***

As they neared Darantha, Jory alerted General Frey of the Gantian fighters headed their way.

"We see them," General Frey said. "We're launching all squadrons as we speak."

"We're all on our way back, too," Jory told him. "It looks like that battle near Ganta Zay was just a diversion so they could send out their fighters."

They could already see the ships engaged in battle. Jory wanted to land and get into his fighter, but there was no opportunity to do so. They'd have to do their fighting in Evalycer's ship.

"At least it's got fire power," Evalycer said. "Though it's straining to keep up with these maneuvers we're trying to do."

"Make sure you hit the cockpit in the glass," Jory told the squadrons. "Otherwise it's just wasted laser-fire. That duratatium is too strong to penetrate."

The RPF out-flew the Gantian fighters with the use of their abilities. Even in Evalycer's ship, she and Jory were able to miss colliding with several ships and evade laser fire.

***

"Darantha's pilots are too good," one of the pilots reported to Keedu.

"You need to keep them occupied as long as you can," Keedu said. "We're about to land."

"Yes, sir," the pilot replied.

Keedu turned to Garrick. "They're getting slaughtered out there," he said as he watched his ships on the ships screen. "Even with the duratatium, they've figured out a way to disable the ships."

Garrick could see that the RPF ships were better than theirs, especially the pilots' flying skills. Ganta Zay's pilots hadn't yet figured out how to use their new-found abilities to fly their ships as the RPF have and were definitely at a disadvantage.

"It won't be for much longer," Garrick said. He punched in another code, and General Frey's face appeared on the screen.

"What do you want, Garrick?' the general asked.

"There is one way to stop this fighting," Garrick said.

"How's that?" the general asked.

"Agree to start shipping the Elixir to Ganta Zay."

"That will never happen," Frey said firmly. "You've shown that you cannot handle the effects of it, and most of your men cannot control what abilities they do have. No negotiations."

"If that's the way you want it," Garrick said, and he disengaged the communicator.

Still cloaked, they landed in an open area near the RPF base. The men pulled on their coats and hoods before stepping off the ship. With Garrick leading the way, looking like travelers, they headed toward the base.

They walked to the outskirts of the base, where it was minimally guarded. The fence that surrounded the base at this point was only monitored with a camera surveillance. They hid behind a rock formation until the camera had panned past their point. Sayzan ran out and started to cut the fence. Once the hole was big enough, Garrick and Keedu ran over and through the hole and onto the base.

That part of the base held old vehicles and other junk that wasn't needed anymore except for scrap parts. As the camera panned back their way, they hid behind an old ship until the camera had passed them. They continued to the building.

"How do we get in?" Keedu whispered.

"We go around to where they keep their vehicles," Garrick said. "We should be able to get in through there."

They walked quietly around to the vehicle area. There were a few men there, working on various vehicles and ships. Garrick nodded his head in their direction, creating a disturbance on the opposite side. The mechanics turned their attention toward the sound, and Garrick, Keedu, and Sayzan ran inside the building.

"Do you know where to look for the princess?" Sayzan asked.

"Yes, I do," Garrick said. "I heard her talking once on Foridian, telling Governor Oxmoor where her office was situated on the base. It shouldn't be hard to find."

They walked through the vehicle area, staying close to the sides in the shadows and behind the vehicles there. Garrick stretched out with his ability to see ahead of them, searching the corridors for people. When the corridor was clear, they walked quickly through it and around the corner to a stairwell.

"We have to go up one floor," Garrick said. He checked the stairwell and found it empty. They proceeded up to the next floor to the main level of the base, over the hangar bay. The control center buzzed with activity, as Garrick knew it would because of the battle. With everything going on, Garrick hoped that they would not be noticed as they made their way across the room to Princess Maryllia's office.

Once safely across, they went down the short corridor to the princess's office. Garrick opened the door and found it empty.

"Damn it!" Keedu exclaimed. "Where do we look now?"

"She'll returned eventually," Garrick said, sitting in a chair and putting his feet up on the desk. "We'll wait for her."

They didn't have to wait for very long, as the princess came in a few minutes later. She initially didn't see anyone in her office, as she was looking down at her tablet. When she looked up and saw Garrick sitting there, she dropped her tablet and reached for her weapon, but Garrick was faster and pulled it from her hand using his ability. It fell onto her desk. She turned and tried to run, but her leg was still healing and Keedu caught up to her and grabbed her from behind.

"Stop struggling, princess, or I'll snap your neck," Keedu said. She stopped moving.

"What the hell do you want now?" she asked.

"You, of course," Keedu said. "We were very displeased with the way you started trouble with me and Sayzan."

"That's what this is about?" she said incredulously. "You're still mad about that?"

Keedu tightened his hold on Maryllia. She gagged and coughed, pulling at Keedu's arm across her neck.

"Don't hurt her just yet, Keedu," Garrick said calmly. "We're going to need her to teach us more about using our abilities."

Keedu relaxed his hold slightly, but still had her in a headlock.

Garrick moved closer to Maryllia. "You're going to come with us without any trouble, or we'll kill you now."

Maryllia said nothing.

"I will take by your silence that you agree. We're going to walk calmly out across the room and out the hangar bay. You do anything and I'll make sure we don't miss with that chemical laser."

Sayzan showed Maryllia the blaster hanging at his side. Again she said nothing.

"Good. Let's go."

Keedu let go of Maryllia with a shove, throwing her off balance. She fell into the wall, steadied herself and led the way out from her office. Everyone seemed too occupied with what they were doing to notice the group walking past them.

"Lieutenant Vance," someone called to her. "We need your help with this…"

Keedu shot the young man in the leg with the regular blaster. The sound made everyone stop and look toward them. Garrick grabbed Maryllia from behind, holding his knife to her throat. Everyone with a weapon turned and aimed their weapon at the three men.

"Anyone gets any closer, and she dies," Garrick shouted.

General Frey came to the front as the group started to surround Garrick and his men.

"No one will come any closer, Garrick," Frey said, holding his hands out to everyone to stay back. No one lowered their weapon, however.

"Just let us go and no one will have to get hurt," Garrick said.

"Why do you want to take Lieutenant Vance?" the general asked. "What use is she to you?"

"We still need her to teach us, the Gantians, how to get full use of our abilities," Garrick said, fully admitting his background. "Plus, I'm not happy with her for trying to cause contention between Keedu and Sayzan. She will pay for that as well."

Chapter Twenty-Seven

"Major Vance," came a voice over the headset. Jory didn't recognize the voice, and they weren't calling this ship, they were calling *him*. "This is Sergeant Netbaum. We have a situation here at the base."

"What's going on?" Jory asked.

"Gantians have come onto the base and they have your sister. Major Needham instructed me to contact you to tell you."

"What?" he exclaimed. "How did they get on base?"

"We don't know, sir," Netbaum replied. "General Frey is talking to them right now."

"Is Maryllia hurt?" Jory asked.

"No, they haven't hurt her. I don't know what is happening out there right now."

"Thank you for contacting me. Vance out."

He stared out into space for a moment, then turned to Evalycer, who was watching him.

"We've got to think of a way to help them," Jory said.

Evalycer turned her ship toward Darantha. "We'll head that way and think of something while we go," she said.

They landed near the base and Jory ran onto the base, Tobias and Evalycer following.

More slowly, but still with urgency, the three of them went through the hangar bay and upstairs to the control room, keeping to the sides, out of sight. As they got closer to the control room, they could see the crowd of people standing grouped together, looking toward Garrick and Maryllia. Jory could hear General Frey talking to Garrick, trying to negotiate with him. They managed to go around them all without being seen, coming up a little behind and to the right of them. Jory, Tobias, and Evalycer each pulled out their blasters and aimed at Garrick.

"Drop it, Garrick," Jory shouted.

Keedu and Sayzan turned their weapons onto the three of them. Garrick turned slightly, still keeping the knife at Maryllia's throat.

"If it isn't Prince Jordan, here to save the day, again," Garrick said, smiling coldly.

"I guess I'm a glutton for punishment," he joked, but his eyes were dead-serious. "Let her go."

"General Frey has been asking me to do the same thing," Garrick replied. "But I need her for a few things back on Ganta Zay."

The knife in Garrick's hand twitched, but stayed put. "That's not going to work," Garrick said. "I can block any attempts to hurt or disarm me."

"What?" Jory said, surprised. "I've never heard of anyone being able to do that."

"I've learned quite a few tricks because of the Elixir."

Jory tried to inflict pain on Garrick, but he only made him flinch.

"That one doesn't work, either, your highness. As I said, I can block any attempts to hurt me, too."

"Look around you, Garrick," General Frey said. "You're not getting out of here with Lieutenant Vance. There are probably thirty blasters aimed at you right now. Do you like your odds?"

"I do, because if anyone tries anything, Sayzan's got the chemical blaster. You remember that one, don't you, princess?"

Maryllia nodded.

"We're going to take the princess with us, and we'll see about returning her later," Garrick said.

Jory said, "Now!" in his head, and Evalycer shot at Sayzan but missed. Sayzan aimed the chemical blaster at Evalycer, hitting her in her left arm. She cried out, more from anger than pain. She shot at Sayzan again, this time hitting him in the chest and he fell to the floor.

Keedu started to run down the corridor, but Tobias shot him, killing him.

Garrick started down the same hallway, pulling Maryllia with him. Jory saw Maryllia struggling against his grip, but with Garrick's strength ability, she couldn't get away from him. Jory ran after them and fired his blaster, hitting Garrick in the right leg. He released his grip on Maryllia as he fell to the floor and grabbed his leg. Maryllia turned and kicked Garrick in the stomach as Jory ran up with his blaster aimed at Garrick.

"I don't need to use my abilities to cause you pain," Maryllia said angrily.

"Like General Frey said," Jory panted. "You're not getting out of here with my sister."

Jory handed his blaster to Maryllia, who aimed it at Garrick. Jory pulled Garrick up from the floor and held Garrick's hands behind his back and marched him into the control room.

General Frey turned to see Jory and Maryllia bring Garrick in as the rest of the troops applauded. Frey motioned for four security guards to take Garrick to the holding cell. The put binders on his wrists and checked for other weapons.

Evalycer had gone to the medical bay to have the chemical cut out of her flesh and repair the damage. General Frey sent Maryllia to the medical bay to be checked over as well, then turned to the control panel. He pressed a button and said, "Attention Gantian fighters: Keedu is dead and Garrick is in our custody. Surrender at once, or be prepared to be destroyed."

"What do you mean, Keedu is dead?" one of the pilots replied. "I want proof!"

One of the technicians used his communicator to send video to the Gantian fighters. He first showed Garrick in binders, and then panned over to show Keedu dead on the ground, along with Sayzan.

"There is your proof," Frey said. "You will retreat, or I will send out every pilot I have to annihilate your squadrons."

A few moments later, the technician declared that all the Gantian fighters were pulling away. Deafening applause and cheers arose from the control room. General Frey shook Jory's hand, then Jory ran to the medical bay to check on Evalycer and Maryllia.

Jory found Maryllia sitting on a table, one of the medics checking over her injuries. After making sure she was okay, Jory then went to the surgical unit. He watched the doctor work on Evalycer's left arm, carefully cutting away the chemical and cleaning the wound. Once that was done, he applied medication to the wound to help it heal, bandaged her arm and moved her into the recovery room.

"You can see her in about an hour," the doctor told Jory. "She'll be fine in a couple of days."

"Thank you," Jory said, and he left to speak to General Frey.

Tobias was in General Frey's office, as well as Fletcher and Yates.

"Well done, all of you," Frey said.

"Thank you, sir," Jory said.

"I've contacted Governor Oxmoor to let him know of the events of today," the general said. "He's very pleased with the outcome. He would like all of us to attend a reception the day after tomorrow to celebrate. He wanted to do it tomorrow, but I told him that Lieutenant Nichols wouldn't be well enough by then. She needs to be there, too."

"Absolutely," Jory agreed.

After the debriefing, Jory went to see Garrick in the detention area of the base. Garrick sat on the bench in the small room, behind reinforced glass. Though he'd been beaten, he still had the smug look on his face.

"You may as well get used to this view," Jory told him. "I expect it won't change much once you're sent back to Foridian."

"I don't plan on going back there," Garrick said. "I plan on escaping."

"I'd like to see you try, Garrick. By tomorrow, your abilities will have diminished to next to nothing. There will be a force field around your cell tonight as well. You will not be able to use your abilities on anyone through it. I'd say your chances are pretty slim." Garrick said nothing, but Jory noticed that he became a little less complacent. His face lost its arrogance and his eyes darted around the room. "I see you're getting the hint now. Guess who is taking you back to Foridian? Me, of course, and my co-pilot, Captain Kelly. Evalycer will also be joining us, and my sister. The best of the best. There is no way in hell you are escaping from us."

With that, Jory left Garrick to agonize over that information. Jory went back to check on Evalycer.

"She's not awake," the nurse said. "But you can go in and sit with her."

Jory went into the room and pulled the chair over next to Evalycer's bed. "What a hell of a few days it's been, huh?" he said quietly.

"It sure beats the boring runs I used to do," Evalycer whispered. She opened her eyes and smiled at Jory.

"Hey, you *are* awake," he said.

"It's going to take more than a little laser blast to keep me down."

"Yeah, some laser blast," he said.

He got her up to speed on the events for the next couple of days. "It will be very satisfying to see Garrick in binders as we take him back to Foridian," Jory said.

"I can't wait," Evalycer said. She touched her bandaged shoulder. "At least I got the satisfaction of killing Sayzan."

Jory left a few minutes later to let Evalycer rest. He saw Maryllia for a few minutes before checking out of the base and heading home to Samara. It seemed so long since he had seen her. The whole Elixir trade had not gone as planned.

Samara smiled as Jory came in through the door of her office. She stood up and gave Jory a long welcome home kiss, and hugged him tightly to her, never wanting to let him go.

"I'm so glad you're home and in one piece," she said.

"It's been a hell of a project," Jory replied.

Over dinner, Jory told Samara everything that had happened. She felt a little guilty about what had happened with Garrick.

"I saw that he was learning everything quickly," she started. "But it didn't occur to me that he was getting stronger than everyone else."

"He hid it well," Jory said. "At least for a while, and you never saw how aggressive he became. That was the scary part, how aggressive and unstable they turned out to be."

After dinner, Jory climbed into bed with his wife, pulling her close to him, her back to his front. He kissed the back of her neck, wrapping his arm around her waist. It was the most relaxed he'd felt in a long time.

After breakfast the next morning, Jory drove to the base hospital to check in on Evalycer. When he got to her room, he found her sitting up in bed, eating her breakfast.

"You look a lot better today," Jory said with a smile.

"I feel better," Evalycer said. "I'm trying to get them to discharge me today so I can check my ship before tomorrow."

"Tobi and I can check it out for you."

"Thanks, that'd help a lot. What's the plan with taking Garrick back to Foridian?"

"It should be a straight shot there, no hassles or anything."

"Yeah, I'll believe that when I see it," she said.

Jory told her he'd see her later and went out to the hangar bay to find Tobias. He found him in the control room, going over his report on his tablet.

226

"I told Evalycer we'd go over her ship for her while she's recuperating," Jory told him.

Tobias turned off the tablet. "Sure, let's check it over."

They looked over the engines to make sure there were no lasting problems from the pulse beam that had taken out the hyperdrive and cloaking device. Tobias's and Evalycer's repairs had held. The weapons looked good. They were finishing up as Evalycer came over, her left arm in a sling.

"Hey, they released you," Jory said.

"I told them they had to," Evalycer said. "Otherwise, I'd make a big stink about it until they did. They did tell me to take it easy for the rest of the day."

"No restrictions on flying?" Jory asked.

"Yeah," she admitted. "But I told him that I had to fly tomorrow to take Garrick back. I can go, but I'm not allowed to pilot the ship. So that will fall to you two."

"Not a problem," Jory said. "Between you and Maryllia, I think Garrick will be in good hands."

Evalycer's com beeped. She pulled it off her belt to look at it. "General Frey wants to see me," she said. "I think I know what this is about."

"Want me to go with you?" Jory asked.

"No. I'll face the music alone. It's my responsibility."

***

Evalycer knocked on the office door. General Frey called her in. She took a deep breath before opening the door.

"Take a seat," General Frey said.

Evalycer sat in front of his desk and looked up expectantly.

"I think you know why you're here," Frey started.

"Yes, sir," she said.

"Knowingly putting the Royal family in danger is considered treason. You could go to prison for a long time for that."

"Yes, sir," Evalycer said. Her RPF training had kicked in, replying respectfully and only to what he said. She didn't want to get into more trouble than she was already in.

"I've spoken with Major Vance again on this issue, who in turn spoke with Lieutenant Vance. She had to be informed of this. They've agreed to not press any charges against you. Major Vance suggested that you've been through enough punishment in dealing with the Gantians and being held hostage on Ganta Zay. He says that you went above and beyond with helping Lieutenant Vance when she was shot with the chemical weapon.

"Major Vance has a very high opinion of you," Frey continued. "And Lieutenant Vance also speaks highly of you. I took everything they said under consideration. I wish you had come to me before this happened to tell me so we could have started going around Jenubri from the beginning."

"I know it was wrong, sir," she said, finally speaking up. "I was scared and really didn't know what to do. I take full responsibility for what happened."

"It was their request that nothing be done. I agree that you have been put through a lot these past few weeks." He paused, and looked at Evalycer. His face changed from being a general to looking almost fatherly. She had never seen him look so kind. "You have a couple of good friends, Miss Nicholls. You must have shown great loyalty to them through all this. I hope you appreciate what they've done for you."

Evalycer smiled. "I do," she said.

"We'll see you tomorrow," General Frey said. "Dismissed."

Evalycer stood and shook hands with General Frey, then turned and left.

Jory looked up when she approached him and Tobias in the hangar bay.

"How'd it go?" he asked.

"I think you know," she said, smiling warmly. She hugged Jory with her right arm, patting him on the back. "Thank you for what you did for me," she said, stepping back to look him in his face.

"I'm sorry I had to tell Maryllia," he said. "But she needed to know the entire story so she would agree with me."

"It's okay," she said. "It's time to face up to that as well."

She told Jory and Tobias that she'd see them in the morning, and left to go home, but not before finding Maryllia to thank her for her support.

"Like I told General Frey, I trust you," Maryllia said. "You've always been a good officer and you've been a good friend, too."

Evalycer hugged Maryllia quickly before heading home.

***

Maryllia sat at her desk in her office, going over a few minor security items for her department. Someone knocked on her door and she beckoned them in.

"Hey," Jory said, poking his head around the door. "Have a minute?"

"Of course," she said.

Jory came in and slid into the chair in front of her desk.

"What I want to know is how did the best interrogator in the fleet get fooled by Garrick?"

Maryllia set down her stylus, pushed her tablet out of the way, and folded her hands on her desk.

"I've thought about that," she said. "I read Garrick's mind that one time on Vista at the conference. I didn't see anything to be concerned with at that time, so I never had any reason to read it again after that."

"What about his alter-ego Garson?"

"I wasn't in his presence at any time when I was held on Ganta Zay. I always got a strange feeling from Garrick when we delivered the shipments, but since I'd already read his mind, I didn't think to do it again. I wish I had, but I just thought he was stressed, same as Oxmoor. I wasn't fooled, I just had no reason to suspect him. When I read Keedu's mind, I wasn't looking for anything about Garrick or Garson. I was focused on finding out things to get Sayzan and Keedu angry with each other."

"Well, glad to see that I won't have to recommend a demotion," Jory said with a mischievous grin.

Maryllia picked up the stylus and threw it at her brother, hitting him in his left shoulder.

"For that, I might have to, though," he laughed, rising to his feet.

He hugged his sister, happy that she was healing from her ordeal. He gave her a playful nudge to her arm as he turned and left to go home.

Chapter Twenty-Eight

The next morning, the security team led Malin Garrick out to the ship in ankle binders and his hands bound behind him. Jory took pleasure in seeing Garrick in that position. He'd caused so much grief for them, Jory wasn't even sorry when Garrick tripped and fell as security guided him up the ramp onto the ship.

Maryllia, wearing her full weapon array, looked strong and determined as she put Garrick into the cargo hold and strapped him into a seat back there. She patted him rather roughly on the cheek and told him, "Enjoy your flight."

Evalycer came onboard, also wearing her weapons belt. Despite having her arm in a sling, she could still pull out her blaster and use it, if needed.

"Base, this is Tyrian One," Jory said into the headset.

"Go ahead."

"We are ready to take off and get this scum off our planet."

"You're cleared to take off," the base said.

"Copy that," Jory said, and he and Tobias started the engines and were airborne and on their way to Foridian.

They got to the asteroid belt and followed the security team through the asteroids. Once through, they went light speed to Foridian. They requested to land at the base there, and once on the ground, Jory spoke with Governor Oxmoor, who met them at the base.

"Garrick is all yours," Jory said.

"Thank you," Oxmoor replied. "He will be put on trial and sentenced for all the things he's done, both to us and to you and your planet."

They turned to see Maryllia and Evalycer bringing Garrick down the ramp. His head hanging down, shoulders slumped over, and if it was even possible, looking paler than ever, he looked like a man who had lost everything.

Oxmoor's security guards took Garrick from Maryllia and Evalycer and led him to their detention cells below the control room.

General Frey, Fletcher, Yates, and several other pilots arrived later that afternoon for the reception for all of them for capturing Garrick and killing Keedu and Sayzan. After dinner, Governor Oxmoor stood up to speak.

"I just wanted to say 'thank you' to everyone for the successful capture of Malin Garrick," Oxmoor started. "Without their help, we wouldn't be receiving the Elixir anymore. Special thanks for Major Jordan Vance, Lieutenant Maryllia Vance, Lieutenant Tobias Kelly, and Evalycer Nicholls for all the work they put into ending this battle."

Everyone applauded. Tobias, and Maryllia stood up quickly, but Jory and Evalycer were more subdued. Although used to the attention, Jory still wanted to just stay in the background. He looked at Evalycer, whose wide-eyed glance around at everyone told him she felt the same.

"Do I really have to stand?" she whispered.

"You knew this moment was going to come," he said.

"So did you," she chuckled.

"Let's get this over with, then we can go home."

Jory and Evalycer finally stood. Jory waved his hand at the crowd while Evalycer curtly nodded her head in acknowledgement.

After the reception, they all flew back to Darantha. Having nothing else to do until the following week when the next shipment of Elixir would be made, Evalycer said she was going home and not doing anything until then.

"I think I've earned the right to do absolutely nothing," she joked.

Jory and Samara met with Tobias and his fiancée for a late dinner that evening. It had been a long time since the friends had been able to do so.

***

The next week, Evalycer was back at the base, healed from her injury and ready to pick up the shipment to Foridian. She found Jory and Tobias already in the hangar bay, waiting on her and Maryllia.

"Do you really think we need an escort now?" she asked.

"I don't want to take any chances with this, just yet," Jory said.

After the hangar crew had loaded the shipment onto the *Silver Reign*, Jory and his team were on their way to Foridian. They arrived at the asteroid belt and called the security patrol to help them through. Once past the field, they flew cautiously past Ganta Zay. All seemed quiet as they passed through, no activity of any kind from Ganta Zay.

As the Foridian crew unloaded the shipment, Governor Oxmoor spoke with Jory.

"Next week will be the last week you'll need to bring the Elixir to us," Oxmoor said. "Our facility will be up and running the week after next."

"That is excellent news," Jory said. Evalycer looked a little unhappy about that news.

When Oxmoor left, Jory turned to Evalycer. "What's wrong?"

"Once this is done, I'll be out of a job again," she said.

"Aren't they going to have you deliver the plant to Foridian?"

"I haven't been approached about it yet. I never assume anything."

"I'll talk to General Frey about it," he told her.

Her mood brightened considerably. "Thanks, I appreciate it."

With the Elixir unloaded, they headed back to Darantha.

Back at the base, Jory spoke with General Frey about keeping Evalycer on the route to Foridian. "She's eager to keep doing it," he told the general.

"I thought she'd want to go do something on her own," the general said.

"I think she just wants to know what her next job is," Jory replied.

"I had thought about letting her go, since her contract was just to deliver the Elixir. You and your sister convinced me to keep her. If you can trust her, I can, too."

"She wasn't trying to put us into harm's way, she was just trying to keep herself safe."

"We'll keep her on the route, if that's what she wants."

"I'll let her know."

Jory found Evalycer a little later, working on her ship.

"I spoke with General Frey," Jory started. "He said he'll keep you on the route to deliver the Elixir plants to Foridian."

Evalycer smiled. "Great! I thought he'd let me go after the Startia fiasco."

"He did say that he thought about it, but that was before Maryllia and I talked to him."

"I appreciate what you and Maryllia have done for me, putting your trust in me."

"You may as well re-up and work with us here on the base, as much as you're going to be here," Jory joked.

"No way in hell will that will ever happen," Evalycer said. "Rules are not for me."

Jory laughed, then waved goodbye to her. He went back home to relax with his wife, and enjoy the calm of the galaxy, for now.

Thank you so much for reading The Elixir Deception, book two in The Elixir series. If you enjoyed it, please consider leaving a review on Amazon or Goodreads and tell your friends about it! If you found any typos, please email me at jedi_anegram@hotmail.com.

I love space operas and fantasies and grew up watching Star Wars. I was mesmerized when I saw A New Hope back in 1977 for the first time and then spent a lot of my babysitting money to see The Empire Strikes Back many times over. I will watch every Star Wars film until they stop making them. I'm also a die-hard Harry Potter fan—both the books and the movies (I'm sorted into Gryffindor). I just like to be taken away as I read books and watch movies.

I'd like to thank the writer communities I'm a part of, both online and here in Colorado. Aspiring Authors, Ink Authors, Sparkly Badgers of Facebook, SciFi Roundtable have all given me a wealth of knowledge and help anytime I ask. Pikes Peak Writers has been a great help with their yearly conference and monthly Write Brains. I love to learn and will probably never learn all there is about this writing stuff, but I'll have fun trying!

Feel free to Like my Facebook page www.facebook.com/AuthorMargenaAdamsHolmes

Other books by Margena Adams Holmes
On The Line
Dark Harmony
The Elixir War
Dear Moviegoer: Tales From Behind The Velvet Curtains

www.ingramcontent.com/pod-product-compliance
Lightning Source LLC
Chambersburg PA
CBHW050036180626
46810CB00002B/754